SUSAN SCA
CLOTHES-Pі

Susan Scarlett is a pseudonym of the author Noel
Streatfeild (1895-1986). She was born in Sussex,
England, the second of five surviving children of
William Champion Streatfeild, later the Bishop of
Lewes, and Janet Venn. As a child she showed an
interest in acting, and upon reaching adulthood sought
a career in theatre, which she pursued for ten years, in
addition to modelling. Her familiarity with the stage
was the basis for many of her popular books.

Her first children's book was *Ballet Shoes* (1936),
which launched a successful career writing for
children. In addition to children's books and memoirs,
she also wrote fiction for adults, including romantic
novels under the name 'Susan Scarlett'. The twelve
Susan Scarlett novels are now republished by Dean
Street Press.

Noel Streatfeild was appointed an Officer of the Order
of the British Empire (OBE) in 1983.

ADULT FICTION BY NOEL STREATFEILD

As Noel Streatfeild

The Whicharts (1931)

Parson's Nine (1932)

Tops and Bottoms (1933)

A Shepherdess of Sheep (1934)

It Pays to be Good (1936)

Caroline England (1937)

Luke (1939)

The Winter is Past (1940)

I Ordered a Table for Six (1942)

Myra Carroll (1944)

Saplings (1945)

Grass in Piccadilly (1947)

Mothering Sunday (1950)

Aunt Clara (1952)

Judith (1956)

The Silent Speaker (1961)

As Susan Scarlett
(All available from Dean Street Press)

Clothes-Pegs (1939)

Sally-Ann (1939)

Peter and Paul (1940)

Ten Way Street (1940)

The Man in the Dark (1940)

Babbacombe's (1941)

Under the Rainbow (1942)

Summer Pudding (1943)

Murder While You Work (1944)

Poppies for England (1948)

Pirouette (1948)

Love in a Mist (1951)

SUSAN SCARLETT

CLOTHES-PEGS

With an introduction
by Elizabeth Crawford

DEAN STREET PRESS

A Furrowed Middlebrow Book

FM85

Published by Dean Street Press 2022

First published in 1939 by Hodder & Stoughton

Cover by DSP

ISBN 978 1 915393 08 1

www.deanstreetpress.co.uk

INTRODUCTION

WHEN reviewing *Clothes-Pegs*, Susan Scarlett's first novel, the *Nottingham Journal* (4 April 1939) praised the 'clean, clear atmosphere carefully produced by a writer who shows a rich experience in her writing and a charm which should make this first effort in the realm of the novel the forerunner of other attractive works'. Other reviewers, however, appeared alert to the fact that *Clothes-Pegs* was not the work of a tyro novelist but one whom *The Hastings & St Leonards Observer* (4 February 1939) described as 'already well-known', while explaining that this 'bright, clear, generous work', was 'her first novel of this type'. It is possible that the reviewer for this paper had some knowledge of the true identity of the author for, under her real name, Noel Streatfeild had, as the daughter of the one-time vicar of St Peter's Church in St Leonards, featured in its pages on a number of occasions.

By the time she was reincarnated as 'Susan Scarlett', Noel Streatfeild (1897-1986) had published six novels for adults and three for children, one of which had recently won the prestigious Carnegie Medal. Under her own name she continued publishing for another 40 years, while Susan Scarlett had a briefer existence, never acknowledged by her only begetter. Having found the story easy to write, Noel Streatfeild had thought little of *Ballet Shoes*, her acclaimed first novel for children, and, similarly, may have felt Susan Scarlett too facile a writer with whom to be identified. For Susan Scarlett's stories were, as the *Daily Telegraph* (24 February 1939) wrote of *Clothes-Pegs*, 'definitely unreal, delightfully impossible'. They were fairy tales, with realistic backgrounds, categorised as perfect 'reading for Black-out nights' for the 'lady of the house' (*Aberdeen Press and Journal*, 16 October 1939). As Susan Scarlett, Noel Streatfeild was able to offer daydreams to her readers, exploiting her varied experiences and interests to create, as her publisher advertised, 'light, bright, brilliant present-day romances'.

Noel Streatfeild was the second of the four surviving children of parents who had inherited upper-middle class values and expectations without, on a clergy salary, the financial means of realising them. Rebellious and extrovert, in her childhood and youth she had found many aspects of vicarage life unappealing, resenting both the restrictions thought necessary to ensure that a vicar's daughter behaved in a manner appropriate to the family's status, and the genteel impecuniousness and unworldliness that deprived her of, in particular, the finer clothes she craved. Her lack of scholarly application had unfitted her for any suitable occupation, but, after the end of the First World War, during which she spent time as a volunteer nurse and as a munition worker, she did persuade her parents to let her realise her dream of becoming an actress. Her stage career, which lasted ten years, was not totally unsuccessful but, as she was to describe on *Desert Island Discs*, it was while passing the Great Barrier Reef on her return from an Australian theatrical tour that she decided she had little future as an actress and would, instead, become a writer. A necessary sense of discipline having been instilled in her by life both in the vicarage and on the stage, she set to work and in 1931 produced *The Whicharts*, a creditable first novel.

By 1937 Noel was turning her thoughts towards Hollywood, with the hope of gaining work as a scriptwriter, and sometime that year, before setting sail for what proved to be a short, unfruitful trip, she entered, as 'Susan Scarlett', into a contract with the publishing firm of Hodder and Stoughton. The advance of £50 she received, against a novel entitled *Peter and Paul*, may even have helped finance her visit. However, the Hodder costing ledger makes clear that this novel was not delivered when expected, so that in January 1939 it was with *Clothes-Pegs* that Susan Scarlett made her debut. For both this and *Peter and Paul* (January 1940) Noel drew on her experience of occasional employment as a model in a fashion house, work for which, as she later explained, tall, thin actresses were much in demand in the 1920s.

Both *Clothes-Pegs* and *Peter and Paul* have as their settings Mayfair modiste establishments (Hanover Square and Bruton Street respectively), while the second Susan Scarlett novel, *Sally-Ann* (October 1939) is set in a beauty salon in nearby Dover Street. Noel was clearly familiar with establishments such as this, having, under her stage name 'Noelle Sonning', been photographed to advertise in *The Sphere* (22 November 1924) the skills of M. Emile of Conduit Street who had 'strongly waved and fluffed her hair to give a "bobbed" effect'. *Sally-Ann* and *Clothes-Pegs* both feature a lovely, young, lower-class 'Cinderella', who, despite living with her family in, respectively, Chelsea (the rougher part) and suburban 'Coulsden' (by which may, or may not, be meant Coulsdon in the Croydon area, south of London), meets, through her Mayfair employment, an upper-class 'Prince Charming'. The theme is varied in *Peter and Paul* for, in this case, twins Pauline and Petronella are, in the words of the reviewer in the *Birmingham Gazette* (5 February 1940), 'launched into the world with jobs in a London fashion shop after a childhood hedged, as it were, by the vicarage privet'. As we have seen, the trajectory from staid vicarage to glamorous Mayfair, with, for one twin, a further move onwards to Hollywood, was to have been the subject of Susan Scarlett's debut, but perhaps it was felt that her initial readership might more readily identify with a heroine who began the journey to a fairy-tale destiny from an address such as '110 Mercia Lane, Coulsden'.

As the privations of war began to take effect, Susan Scarlett ensured that her readers were supplied with ample and loving descriptions of the worldly goods that were becoming all but unobtainable. The novels revel in all forms of dress, from underwear, 'sheer triple ninon step-ins, cut on the cross, so that they fitted like a glove' (*Clothes-Pegs*), through daywear, 'The frock was blue. The colour of hare-bells. Made of some silk and wool material. It had perfect cut.' (*Peter and Paul*), to costumes, such as 'a brocaded evening coat; it was almost military in cut, with squared shoulders and a little tailored collar, very tailored at the waist, where it went in to flare out to the floor' (*Sally-Ann*), suitable to wear while dining at the Berkeley or the Ivy, establishments to which her heroines – and her readers – were introduced. Such details and the satisfying plots, in which innocent loveliness triumphs against the machinations of Society beauties, did indeed prove popular. Initial print runs of 2000 or 2500 soon sold out and reprints and cheaper editions were ordered. For instance, by the time it went out of print at the end of 1943, *Clothes-Pegs* had sold a total of 13,500 copies, providing welcome royalties for Noel and a definite profit for Hodder.

Susan Scarlett novels appeared in quick succession, particularly in the early years of the war, promoted to readers as a brand; 'You enjoyed *Clothes-Pegs*. You will love Susan Scarlett's *Sally-Ann'*, ran an advertisement in the *Observer* (5 November 1939). Both *Sally-Ann* and a fourth novel, *Ten Way Street* (1940), published barely five months after *Peter and Paul*, reached a hitherto untapped audience, each being serialised daily in the *Dundee Courier*. It is thought that others of the twelve Susan Scarlett novels appeared as serials in women's magazines, but it has proved possible to identify only one, her eleventh, *Pirouette*, which appeared, lusciously illustrated, in *Woman* in January and February 1948, some months before its book publication. In this novel, trailed as 'An enthralling story – set against the glittering fairyland background of the ballet', Susan Scarlett benefited from Noel Streatfeild's knowledge of the world of dance, while giving her post-war readers a young heroine who chose a husband over a promising career. For, common to most of the Susan Scarlett novels is the fact that the central figure is, before falling into the arms of her 'Prince Charming', a worker, whether, as we have seen, a Mayfair mannequin or beauty specialist, or a children's nanny, 'trained' in *Ten Way Street*, or, as in *Under the Rainbow* (1942), the untrained minder of vicarage orphans; in *The Man in the Dark* (1941) a paid companion to a blinded motor car racer; in *Babbacombe's* (1941) a department store assistant; in *Murder While You Work* (1944) a munition worker; in *Poppies for England* (1948) a member of a concert party; or, in *Pirouette*, a ballet dancer. There are only two exceptions, the first being the heroine of *Summer Pudding* (1943) who, bombed out of the London office in which she worked, has been forced to retreat to an archetypal southern English village. The other is *Love in a Mist* (1951), the final Susan Scarlett novel, in which, with the zeitgeist returning women to hearth and home, the central character is a housewife and mother, albeit one, an American, who, prompted by a too-earnest interest in child psychology, popular in the post-war years, attempts to cure what she perceives as her four-year-old son's neuroses with the rather radical treatment of film stardom.

Between 1938 and 1951, while writing as Susan Scarlett, Noel Streatfeild also published a dozen or so novels under her own name, some for children, some for adults. This was despite having no permanent home after 1941 when her flat was bombed, and while undertaking arduous volunteer work, both as an air raid warden close to home in Mayfair, and as a provider of tea and sympathy in an impoverished area of south-east London. Susan Scarlett certainly helped with Noel's expenses over this period, garnering, for instance, an advance of £300 for *Love in a Mist*. Although there were to be no new Susan Scarlett novels, in the 1950s Hodder reissued cheap editions of *Babbacombe's*, *Pirouette*, and *Under the Rainbow*, the 60,000 copies of the latter only finally exhausted in 1959.

During the 'Susan Scarlett' years, some of the darkest of the 20th century, the adjectives applied most commonly to her novels were 'light' and 'bright'. While immersed in a Susan Scarlett novel her readers, whether book buyers or library borrowers, were able momentarily to forget their everyday cares and suspend disbelief, for as the reviewer in the *Daily Telegraph* (8 February 1941) declared, 'Miss Scarlett has a way with her; she makes us accept the most unlikely things'.

Elizabeth Crawford

Chapter One

Ethel Brown looked at the clock. Ten past six. Unconsciously her movements slowed. She went on laying the table but there was the leisure in all she did of one who knows they are ahead of time. If there was one thing Ethel Brown did like, it was being ahead of time. She laid the last fork in place then stood a moment looking at the table, at her cloth, napkins and the anemones in the vase in the centre, at the gleam on her glass and china.

"We may have to live simply," she often said, "but I like to feel if the Queen walks in there's nothing to be ashamed of."

As a matter of fact this statement was a cloak for what she really felt. If you have been selling hardware all day or stitching at other people's clothes, you have a right to expect everything very nice at home. Often in the winter when there was nothing to pick in the garden it was a squeeze to buy a few flowers, but she managed.

"They need to see something bright," she would say to herself as she parted with a threepence or sixpence, "all that fighting to get into the train, must be disheartening, nothing like a bit of colour to buck you up."

She went into the kitchen and looked in her gas oven to see how her cottage pie was doing. She was glad it was cottage pie, George was so fond of it. Difficult he was over his food. Standing about all day at Fordwych's seemed to take the appetite from him. No wonder, she often thought, must be hard being assistant manager under a crotchety man like Mr. Earl. Not that even Mr. Earl could find anything to complain of in George, a harder working man never lived nor one who knew more about his job. Her kitchen was a testimony to all George knew about hardware, wonderful stuff he got at wonderful value.

She went back into the other room and peered out of the window. Nasty looking night, half rain and half sleet. She wished she had not let Alfie go to his scout meeting. But he was so set on it, and had promised to run both ways, and he was a good boy about keeping a promise. She wondered if Annabel had managed to catch George's train. She smiled as she thought of it. What a one George was for making a game out of things. Toffee, if Annabel caught the same train as he did all five nights of the week. Not that it was a game really, George liked Annabel to try, it seemed to make all the difference to him to have one of the children to travel up and down with him. But it made a rush for Annabel. They did not knock off to time at Bertna's like they did at Fordwych's. Funny these smart dress-makers, they never seemed to see that laying down what you were working on at six was not the same as having your work put away by six.

Steps came running up the path. Lorna dashed into the hall. Lorna at twelve was one of Ethel Brown's problems. She seemed to go sliding through life with everything happening to her by accident. Nothing that Lorna did ever seemed to be planned and Ethel Brown believed in plans. She did not altogether blame Lorna, who had silly friends, empty-headed girls who giggled. She would often have liked to have told Lorna just what she thought of those friends but she never did. George who hated gigglers sometimes did speak his mind. Ethel was sorry when this happened because she knew it would mean that Lorna would cling the closer to her friends saying "They don't understand me at home." The trouble in dealing with Lorna was that she sprung things on you so unexpectedly that there was no time to make careful decisions. She did it now.

"Mum, me and Lucy and Rachel and some of the others are going round to sing carols to-night. Have you got a torch I could take?"

Ethel played for time.

"Your father won't like you being about the streets so late."

"Well of course if he doesn't care if the heathens are never made Christians."

"What have the heathens to do with you singing carols?"

"The money's for them." There were voices outside, Lorna swung round. "There's Dad, I'll ask him myself."

"Not till supper." Ethel gently pushed her daughter upstairs. "You go and wash and you can ask him when you come down. And don't make a noise mind, Maudie's asleep."

Stitch, stitch went Annabel. Beautifully neat little stitches, but she made them unconsciously, her mind was miles away. Something, perhaps the blue-green stuff on which she was working had taken her back to a holiday at Bournemouth. The Browns always went to Bournemouth for a fortnight in the summer, except the years when there had been a cut at Fordwych's. But the year Annabel was remembering had been quite different to other years, and that was because she had made friends with some children.

"Funny," she thought. "To think of those children now." Why, she couldn't have been more than twelve then. It was years ago and she had hardly thought of them since. Ann and Lisa they had been called, and there had been the baby who had fallen into the sea, which she had rescued. Silly how everybody had praised her for that, it wasn't anything. But it had been lucky because apart from the wrist-watch their father had given her, she had got to know Ann and Lisa.

Different they had been, somehow, from any other girls she knew. It was a conversation with them that the blue-green stuff had brought to mind. A hot day when you could do nothing but bathe and lie about. It was in one of the lying about periods.

"What would you like to do when you're grown up, Annabel?" Lisa asked.

Annabel threw a pebble into the sea.

"Oh, I don't know. Dad thinks perhaps an office."

Ann and Lisa sat up.

"But that isn't what Lisa asked." Ann explained. "She didn't say what will you do, she said what would you like to do. Just imagine you could choose, anything, a film star, or an opera singer, anything."

Annabel visualised this strange possibility. Then she shook her head.

"I wouldn't like anything like that—I just want something to do until I marry then I'll have lots and lots of children."

Ann beat the pebbles in despair.

"Goodness, how awful. Now me—I'm going to be the most famous doctor in the world, and Lisa is going to be a terrific woman flyer. And there's you just wants babies!"

Annabel was sorry her tastes were such a bore; but even to keep the good opinion of Lisa and Ann she could not change them. She didn't want to do anything grand.

Violet, her next-door neighbour at the work-table, dug her in the ribs.

"What are you dreaming about? Do you know it's six o'clock. Aren't you going home?"

Hurriedly Annabel folded the blue-green stuff, and put away her things. Then ran for her hat and coat. No time to loiter if she was to meet Dad at Victoria.

George and Annabel came into the hall. Strange that proudest and fondest of parents, such as George and Ethel, should have missed the fact that in Annabel they had given birth to real beauty. To them Annabel was not beautiful. They admired more Lorna's fair hair and blue eyes, or baby Maude's brown curls. Annabel had straight dark hair, which she wore parted in the centre, a lovely forehead, brown eyes, unusually wide apart, an enchanting nose and a beautifully modelled mouth. But it took a discerning eye to spot her charms. She was tall and at seventeen was still growing and found stooping over her work tiring, so she slouched. She was not earning much and so had few clothes and in any case had many other things she would rather spend her money on. Taking her mother to the pictures, buying a little something extra for the house in the way of sweets or fruit, or better still putting it into the post office. Annabel liked to save, it was nice to think you had money you could lay your hand on when you wanted it.

George hung up his hat on the hall rack, he gave Ethel a grin over his shoulder.

"Look at that. Here's Friday and Annabel not missed the train once. I'll buy the tin of toffees on my way home to-morrow."

Ethel smiled at him affectionately and murmured "Extravagance," but her eyes were on his socks and Annabel's stockings. They would be sure to be damp. But if there was one thing people back from work hated it was to be told to change their stockings and socks.

"You must be cold both of you. I've a lovely fire. You have a warm before you wash. I'll run up and get your shoes and something dry for your feet."

She started up the stairs but George caught her arm. He sniffed.

"Tripe and onions?" She shook her head. George looked at Annabel. "What do you say?"

Annabel sniffed.

"More like steak and onions."

Ethel ran up the stairs.

"You two greedies. Go and have a warm. You'll know what you're eating when you get it." The time of the day Ethel loved above all was after the washing up was done, sitting round before bed. The children turned on the wireless, and George had a pipe, and she, for the first time since she had got up, relaxed. She especially liked Friday nights. George was paid by the month but he had a mind which worked in weeks, so he gave the month's money to Ethel who solemnly paid him a week's wages every Friday night after supper. Such a business he went through. He was a man who liked to know where he stood. He had a collection of little cash boxes. Across each he wrote on stamp paper the purpose of the box. Rent, that was paying off the mortgage on the house. Gas. Electric light. Special. 'Special' covered anything from the four-pence for recharging the wireless battery to the doctor's bill. When each box had received its quota Ethel had her house-keeping money, and George put his lunch and spending money in his pocket.

It was at that moment that Ethel produced her money box. It was a family joke that never grew stale. Seven years ago, before Maude was born, she had seen some green velvet curtains which were just right for the sitting room. They toned perfectly with the wall paper and were just the sort of curtains she had always wanted, and never had. That night she had put her money box on the mantel-piece.

"That's for my curtains. And I'll have them before Christmas, you'll see."

But she had reckoned without the things life could do to you. Fordwych's, which had kept its head up through the worst of the slump, fell on a bad patch and all wages were cut. They had restored the cut now but while it lasted it had been a wretched time, and several little comforts were done away with, and hardly anything went into her box. Then, when Fordwych's were all right again, came Alfie's illness.

The anxiety of those days had been terrible. Those journeys to and fro to the hospital, and the expense had made the anxiety worse. A boy with a leg in plaster could not walk and that meant taxis. There was a little money in the box then, and she had been glad to slip out a half-crown now and again for she did not want to worry George about money, when he had the thought that Alfie might be sent to a sanatorium on his mind. When Alfie's leg got well there had been quite a while when things went smoothly, and her box had grown heavy. Then came the influenza. She would never forget that winter. She had been able to keep up herself, except for one day when she had fainted in the kitchen, but the rest of the family had been very ill. Alfie, of course, always wanted special care, and little Maudie had needed toys to cheer her up, and Lorna had to be sent away, and she did not think George would ever have got rid of his cough if she had not tried that stout and milk. Ethel often laughed to herself at her family believing there was close on two pounds in her box. Two pounds! More like five shillings. Where did they suppose the money for the extra things had come from?

But now life had stopped doing things to them. Nobody was ill, Fordwych's paying properly and Annabel in a steady job.

She held out her box.

"Who's remembering the curtains this week?"

Alfie was fiddling with the wireless. He was still in his scout uniform. He turned and smiled at his mother, fumbling in his pocket.

"Here's a threepence."

Alfie had only fourpence a week pocket-money. The threepenny-bit caused a family sensation.

"Been robbing a bank?" Annabel enquired.

Lorna was spending the evening sulking, for George had utterly forbidden carol-singing.

"More like robbed the church poor box."

George looked at her severely.

"That's no way to talk, my girl. Not even in fun you shouldn't say a thing like that." He glanced at Alfie. "Where did you get it?"

Alfie came over to his mother. He leant over the back of her chair and pushed the threepence in the curtain box.

"Picked it up down the High Street."

Ethel had a lump in her throat. How like Alfie to give her his threepenny-bit. He had so little money, even a small sum like that was a lot to him. How thin his knees were; that scout uniform showed it up. She did wish he would put on a little flesh. All that extra milk and stuff she gave him never seemed to do a bit of good. She patted his hand, then when she was sure she had control of her voice, said quietly: "You spoil your mum."

George was counting the change in his pocket. He selected some silver.

"There you are, old dear." He dropped the coins in her box. "Though it's my belief you've got enough in there already to do the whole house up in velvet."

Annabel went over with some coppers. She laughed.

"I'd like to see us dolled up like that. We'd look like Royalty."

Lorna glared at the curtains.

"I wish you'd hurry, Mum, and get the new ones. These look so shabby, I don't like bringing people in." George took his pipe out of his mouth.

"Never noticed that it's stopped you yet. But if your friends don't find this house good enough for them they can stay away."

Alfie switched off the wireless.

"I wish they would."

Lorna flushed and opened her mouth, but before she had time to speak, Ethel broke in.

"Now then, that's enough bickering. Lorna knows that I'm pleased to welcome her friends just the same as I am for all of you. Now, Alfie and Lorna, bed. I'll be up in a quarter of an hour to give you both a tuck in."

With the departure of the children silence fell on the room, broken only by a click as George did his nightly winding of the clock. Then Annabel laid down the book she was reading. She stretched and yawned. She stooped to kiss her mother.

"Denise Robins is a lovely writer. Funny what a lot of things happen to the girls she knows. I wonder if anything will happen to any of us."

Ethel put her arm around her.

"What sort of things would you like to happen?"

Annabel laughed. "Nothing. I suppose I'll want to marry some day, but with my job and us all here, things couldn't be much nicer."

The door closed. George tapped the tobacco out of his pipe.

"She's a good girl."

"What, Annabel?" Ethel answered her own question. "You're right. Lovely disposition, contented with things the way they are. Funny you'd think now she's growing up she'd want more."

George patted her shoulder.

"That's your upbringing, old lady. Being satisfied with things, not pulling a long face because someone's got something better."

Ethel got up.

"Satisfied!" She nodded at her box on the mantelpiece. "Ever heard of someone who wanted velvet curtains?"

Lorna sat up in bed and hugged her knees. She looked disdainfully at Annabel.

"When I'm grown up I shall not come home from work and go to bed. I'll be taken out by boys."

Annabel glanced round from the dressing-table.

"I don't know any boys," she said good-humouredly.

"You could."

"Could I?" Annabel brushed her hair. "Matter of fact, I don't know I want to."

"Not want to!" Lorna's voice had a frankly disbelieving note.

Annabel brushed in silence for a moment. The mere expression "taken out by boys" made her squirm. And yet why not? All the other girls she knew were taken out by them.

"I expect Mr. Right will come along one day," she explained gently.

"Not if you don't do something about it he won't."

Annabel laughed. She went over to Lorna's bed.

"You think a lot too much about boys, and, anyway, it's time you were asleep. Turn over and I'll tuck you in."

Annabel finished her undressing, said her prayers, got into bed and turned out the light. In the darkness there was a queer smile on her face.

"Taken out by boys!" She thought. "Not she." Not to Lorna nor to anyone would she confide her secret belief. Somewhere in the world was the man she would marry. She knew, as who that read novels and saw films did not, that it was easy to make a mistake and fall in love with the wrong man. But in her was faith that she would not make a mistake: when she met him she would know. In the meanwhile, why waste time with boys? It was nice waiting when you knew it was only a wait and someone was meeting you later on. Still smiling she went to sleep.

CHAPTER TWO

ANNABEL turned into Hanover Square. It was a raw, unpleasant morning, but she did not notice it. It was Saturday, and only two weeks to Christmas. A cutting wind slashed at her, but her mind was on important things, and had no time for mere inconveniences like cold winds. If she got the cardigan Mum wanted there would not be quite enough for the new spade for Dad. It would be better while she was at it to try and get Alfie a really good fountain pen, cheap ones never lasted. It was a pity Lorna wanted those bangles, a shocking waste of good money, but Christmas was Christmas, and she supposed she might as well have what she wanted. Wouldn't Maudie be pleased with the frock. Very lucky she'd been to get that pattern of one the little Princesses wore. Mum would be pleased to think Maudie was dressed the same as the Princesses.

The stairs at Bertna's were crowded with the workroom staff. Miss Bell, the head fitter, was a tartar, and no one dared be a second late. It took Annabel only a moment to hang up her things, put on her overall, comb her hair and take her place at the workroom table.

"Good morning, Annabel." Miss Bell had an unfortunate gift for making even her pleasantries sound as if she was about to put on a judge's black cap.

"Good morning, Miss Bell," Annabel answered mildly.

Violet, the girl on her left, nudged her.

"Proper meadow lady she is this morning. Been carrying on alarming about the seams on Lady Olivia Bartlett's blue velvet."

Margaret, on Annabel's other side, leant over.

"It's her chilblains. You watch her. She can't stand still a second."

Annabel looked at Miss Bell's feet. They certainly were being moved about in a very uneasy fashion. She threaded her needle.

"Poor thing. I'm sorry for her if it's that."

"So'm I," Violet agreed. "But it's not fair to work them off on us; we didn't give them to her."

Margaret sighed.

"Anyway, if she's got to have them, I wish it wasn't at a time when I'm working on something for the Duchess of Sussex." She held out her work and made a face at it. "If I had a bust that size I wouldn't put cloth of gold with red roses to climb over it. Time she's got this on she'll look like the horticultural show."

Annabel, stitching quickly but exquisitely at the bodice of a white satin frock, let her mind drift. Saturday! She would stop on the way home at that man on the corner. Maybe he'd let her have some flowers cheap; he was often glad to on a Saturday. If she could not get flowers, a bit of holly would be bright.

Downstairs in the inner sanctum, the holy of holies of Bertna's, Tania Petoff, the owner, sat at her desk talking to the head saleswoman. Tania was Russian. Her mother had been dimly connected with the Imperial family; her father had a job about the court. With the revolution they had lost everything, and Tania had been brought up in an atmosphere of defeatism in Monaco. But in Tania there was a strain that abhorred defeat. From a small child her cry had been "But do let's try." When she grew up she did try. She married a rich elderly Englishman, not because she wanted to, but because it was the only way to get those necessities—money and a British passport. With unusual tact her husband died within a year of the marriage and left Tania that respectable object, a British widow. But much as she enjoyed being rich, and the freedom to come and go ensured by her new nationality, she was bored. No good saying "Do let's try" when there is nothing to try about. It was then she turned her mind to clothes, and started the business (which in five years became world famous) Bertna's. At the same time she shed her married name of Huggins; though admirable for a passport, it was not a name for a dressmaker. She went back to Petoff.

"There's one comfort," said the saleswoman, "she didn't show the clothes very well."

Tania drew a rabbit on the blotter in front of her.

"All the same, her leaving in a moment like that has put us in a hole. She was lovely, and another girl of her height and colouring won't be easy to find over Christmas. However, we'd better send to the agencies and see what we can get, I suppose." She paused and gave her rabbit a small hat and a cane. "Unless we try a girl who is already on our staff."

"On the staff!" The saleswoman looked puzzled. "All our girls are too short."

Tania jerked her pencil at the ceiling.

"Look higher."

"Not the workroom!" All the abyss between those who stitched and those who sold was in the saleswoman's voice.

"Yes, the workroom." Tania's scorn for shop snobbery was in her inflection. "Up in the workroom we have one of the most beautiful girls I have ever seen. I've a good mind to bring her down and give her a chance."

"Really!" There was deep disapproval in the saleswoman's tone. "What is her name?"

"Brown. Annabel Brown." Tania pressed a bell. "You shall see."

Annabel, deep in her work and her thoughts, was recalled to the room by a nudge from Violet.

"Look! There's Miss Petoff's secretary. Wonder what she wants."

Margaret cut her thread.

"Come to offer you a rise, I expect."

"Look," Violet whispered, "she is talking about one of us. She keeps looking this way. Stitch up, girls, the Bell is coming. I've a nasty feeling somebody is for it."

"Annabel," Miss Bell spoke grimly, "you will go down at once. Miss Petoff wishes to see you."

"Me!" Annabel got up. In her fluster she dropped her scissors and knocked three reels of silk off the table. "Why?"

Miss Bell raised shocked eyebrows.

"That is scarcely for you to question."

Under cover of picking up the silks, Margaret gave Annabel's leg a comforting squeeze.

"Go on down. There's no need to be scared; you haven't done anything. If the Bell's made up lies about you, I'll tread on her chilblains for you."

Annabel had never been inside Tania's room. Why should she? The only people who went in there were the heads of the departments, and perhaps those astounding girls downstairs, who actually saw the customers who were mere names to the workroom. And perhaps sometimes those even more fabulous creatures, the models, who wore clothes of which Annabel joined the seams for five and a half days of every week. As for Tania herself, she knew her by sight, of course, as who in Bertna's did not, but she had never spoken to her and had never expected to speak to her. And now suddenly she was not only in that inner office, but alone with the great Miss Petoff.

"Good morning." Tania nodded at a chair. "Sit down." Annabel never knew how she got in that chair, but she got there somehow, and fixed scared but dutiful eyes on her employer. "You know," Tania went on, "that I keep four girls to show the models."

Of course Annabel knew. Elizabeth, the red-headed one. Freda, who had the lovely fur coat. Bernadette, who showed the tweeds and the workroom said was a bit of a mystery. And the dark Nancy who always looked so proud. There was no more popular topic of conversation in the workroom than the lives of these four.

"Yes," she agreed in a nervous whisper.

"Nancy has left without giving me notice, and I am thinking of trying you in her place."

"Me!" Annabel was so startled she forgot to be shy, and her "Me!" rang out. To turn her, Annabel Brown, into a model. Why, all the models were beautiful. They earned quite a lot of money and went to all the sort of restaurants the customers went to. Miss Petoff could not really mean it. Why her?

Tania laughed.

"Don't look so startled, my dear child. Has no one ever told you that you are very pretty? Of course you'll have a lot to learn. You must straighten that back, and there is a chance that you may not have the gift. Clothes showing is a gift, you know. Now run along, and on Monday morning we'll give you a trial."

The models at Bertna's had a room to themselves. Tania said that showing a dress decently was exhausting work, and so was standing for fittings, and she could not expect her girls to keep lovely unless they had a chance to rest between times. For this purpose she not only provided four arm-chairs, but four armchairs with feet rests. The showroom girls looked with fury at these chairs and said the models were a pampered lot. When Tania heard this she laughed and said to Miss Gale, her second in command:

"My four beauties have ankles worth worrying about. The others have not."

With a large electric fire and a vase of flowers (provided by each girl in turn) the room really looked very cosy. But its cosiness escaped Elizabeth, Bernadette and Freda on Monday morning.

"Ugh!" Freda groaned. "What a filthy morning. And I was late last night. And does my head feel like bursting?"

Bernadette looked at her.

"Better take some of your bromo seltzer. If you have to show the yellow this morning, you'll match it too well."

Elizabeth dragged off her frock, and in nothing but her knickers and brassiere sat down on the floor by the fire. She took off her stockings and warmed her feet.

"Would you two like a bit of good news to cheer you up?"

Bernadette gave her a shrewd glance.

"Good news from you always means a nice cry all round. Let's get it over."

"Well," Elizabeth waggled her toes, "the new model is coming this morning, and who do you think it is?"

"Who?" Freda stopped stirring the bromo seltzer. "Not that cat Sylvia we had for the show?"

"No." Elizabeth paused. "One of the smart, exquisite creatures out of our own workroom."

"The workroom!" Freda choked over her salts.

"In here! A workroom girl a model at Bertna's! I don't believe it."

Elizabeth got up and fetched the very sheer stockings she kept for modelling.

"It's true. Miss Petoff must have gone mad."

Bernadette stretched herself out in her chair. She opened the *Daily Telegraph*.

"I'll tell you why Miss Petoff has picked her."

The other two looked up.

"Why?"

"Because she looks right. I dare say you two have never noticed it, but there are a few good figures outside this room."

Freda sniffed.

"Whatever she looks like we don't want her in here. Something from the workroom. What sauce!"

"That's right." Elizabeth put on her beige satin shoes. "Probably she's like the advertisements. You know, 'even your best friends won't tell you.'"

Miss Gale opened the door.

"Good morning, girls." She held the door wider to admit Annabel. "This is Annabel Brown. Miss Petoff has decided to try her in Nancy's place." She turned to Annabel. "Now take off your things, dear." She looked at Freda. "She is to put on the green and blue chiffon and then come to the showroom. Miss Petoff wants to see how she shows."

Annabel in an agony of shyness heard the door click to behind her. She looked in terror at the three girls. At Elizabeth's pink satin knickers. At Bernadette's crêpe-de-Chine dressing-gown. At Freda's lovely stockings. How was she to undress under those scathing eyes? Everything she had on was clean. But her stockings had only cost two and elevenpence, and had been bought to last. Her shoes were quite nice, but they were of thick leather with sensible heels. She was horribly conscious of a wool vest and buff artificial silk knickers with elastics at the knees. She could not show herself before these three. She would not.

Bernadette laid down her paper.

"Take off your things. What size are your shoes? I've a second pair I can lend you." Then she smiled. "Hurry up, duckie, we shan't bite you."

Annabel gave her a grateful, nervous smile. Then awkwardly began to unbutton her frock. Bernadette had gone to the cupboard to get the shoes, but without looking at them Annabel could feel Freda's and Elizabeth's eyes glued to her. Fumble as she would, the moment came when her frock had to come off. She lifted it over her head. Freda looked at Elizabeth. There was a pause, then a giggle.

Annabel flushed to the roots of her hair. There were tears in her eyes. Then clearly came Bernadette's voice.

"Don't be upset by our abominable manners. As you have probably guessed, we were dragged up all anyhow."

Annabel had never worn a backless frock before. She was ashamed to have to strip to the waist to put it on. But at last she was dressed. She looked anxiously at Bernadette.

"And now?"

"You go to the showroom. Miss Petoff will tell you what to do."

The door shut on Annabel. Bernadette lay down in her chair.

"I've never been particularly vain, but to be in the room with anyone as lovely as that makes me feel as lousy as I probably look."

Elizabeth examined herself in the glass.

"Fancy looking like that over those knickers." She cocked an eye at Freda. "You and I would have bulged. Let's face it."

Annabel kept from her family the news that she was being tried as a model. She was not a person who liked sympathy, and so if she were to fail and return to the workroom the fewer people who knew of her ignominy the better. From her first practice walk round the showroom she saw her chances of being a permanent model were slight. She had no idea until that morning that showing a dress was an art. In the workroom it had always been supposed that if you were sufficiently lovely to make a good clothes peg you received a large salary and lead a life of ease, occasionally broken by a stroll round the showroom. How frighteningly different was the reality. The special walk, one foot before the other to keep the movements smooth. The different manner to assume with each type of garment.

It happened that her lessons corresponded with a busy time at Bertna's. Just before Christmas there were few customers in to buy, but behind the scenes the most intensive designing and making were going on. Tania believed in an early spring shop. "Women," she said, "felt quite different if they had a spring suit hanging in the cupboard." So it was early in the new year that the invitations for her dress show were sent out. Each card embellished by a bouncing lamb, a branch of blossom or a spring flower. Some little drawing to make the customers feel "Goodness, the spring's almost here and me with nothing to wear!"

Every garment designed for the show was made on the model who was to wear it. For hours Bernadette, Elizabeth and Freda stood while pins were fixed and discussions took place. In between these fittings whichever of them was free was expected to give Annabel a lesson. Annabel quite realised they were tired and did not want to be bothered with her, but she wished at the same time they would remember it was not her fault, that being taught in front of a lot of whispering showroom assistants was hard enough anyway without being made nervous by a sarcastic instructor.

Bernadette was the kindest. She would loll against the door and gaze at Annabel with an odd mixture of boredom and amusement. Occasionally she would offer advice.

"That dress has terribly good pockets. Put your hands in them. No good Miss Petoff designing good lines if we don't draw attention to them."

Freda would walk up and down beside her. Her eyes snapping over Annabel's figure.

"You're looking like a sack of coals. That aristocratic slink has been dead for years. Do keep your back straight. Did you think you were going to a funeral in that dress? Miss Petoff designed it to dance in."

"Dance," Annabel stammered. "I can't dance."

"Nobody wants you to. But a quick turn would show the way the bottom is flared, wouldn't it? Besides, you've two hands; how about holding the skirt out just once? No reason to keep its lines a secret."

Elizabeth's method was to whisper to the showroom girls. Annabel was sure the whispers were about her and would get clumsy. Tripping over her feet, and uncertain what to do with her hands.

"What's the matter?" Elizabeth would ask. "Are there lumps in the carpet? Pity to fall over; the clothes never look well like that. By the way, that dress was designed to look smart. I dare say you've never heard the word before, but you can learn."

Often Annabel wished she was back upstairs overcasting seams, work she thoroughly understood. Gossiping with Violet and Margaret. From the angle of the models' room the workroom looked lovable, secure and homely.

On the Tuesday in Christmas week Annabel's courage deserted her and she ran to the models' room in tears. Freda had been giving her a lesson. The garment was a skirt, jumper and coat. The jumper had reversible cuffs and belt. The coat could be worn open, closed, or with a cape. The skirt had a new kind of inverted pleat, which needed careful showing. It was a cold morning and she had a headache. Each bit of that suit had to be shown separately, no special feature forgotten. Freda always frightened Annabel, and this morning, perhaps because of her headache, she was being stupid. Round and round the room she went, every step escorted by Freda.

"This is the third time I have reminded you that coat can be worn three ways. That's right, drop the belt; nothing looks smarter than the model dropping the clothes all over the floor. Of course, I feel sure you know best, and that it's a mistake to show that skirt, but Miss Petoff thinks that pleat rather good. Must give in to her a bit, you know."

Annabel stumbled and boggled and muddled and was thoroughly ashamed of herself. Then, just as she had forgotten the reversible cuffs for the fourth time, she looked up and saw Miss Bell watching. Miss Bell's voice had even more venom than usual.

"I'm afraid my Annabel is giving you trouble, Freda, so you will be glad to hear I want you for a fitting." She turned to Annabel. "The girls in the workroom have been asking how you were getting on. Until this morning I didn't know. Now I do, and I will be sure to tell them."

Only Bernadette was in the models' room when Annabel dashed in.

"I won't go on," she sobbed. "Why should I? I don't want to show the beastly clothes; I never did. It wasn't my idea. I'd much rather go back to the workroom. The girls hate me down here and—"

"When you've had a nice bath of self-pity," Bernadette's voice cut across the room, "you might tell me what the big scene is about."

Annabel flushed. She stopped feeling hysterical, but she was well away with her tears, and they went on dropping off her nose.

"I'm no good at this work," she hiccoughed. "What's the good of keeping me down here wasting everybody's time?"

Bernadette looked at her watch.

"Half-past eleven. Would you like your fate decided this morning?" Annabel nodded. "Then mop up your face and stop snivelling, and I'll ask Miss Petoff to come and see you modelling."

"Oh, but I've got a headache and—"

Bernadette nodded at the cupboard.

"You'll find a bottle of aspirins in my bag."

"Oh, but—" Annabel gasped, searching wildly for an excuse. "I'm so stupid to-day. Worse than I am usually."

Bernadette wandered slowly back from the door. She came over to Annabel and took hold of her shoulders.

"You're an idiot, Annabel Brown. Do you know what's the matter with you? You've got an inferiority complex. Why do you let a couple of nit-wits like Elizabeth and Freda lord it over you?"

Annabel flushed.

"They are so much smarter than me. They're used to things very different to how we have them at home. Not that home isn't nice, only it's different to what they're used to."

Bernadette shook a despairing head.

"My poor sweet. You really must open your eyes a bit wider. Where do you think Elizabeth and Freda live? Buckingham Palace?"

"No, of course not, but I know it's different to us."

"Rubbish! Different my foot! Freda's father is dead and her mother deals in second-hand clothes. Very second-hand, the sort that eventually find their way to barrows. Elizabeth's parents run some sort of boarding-house. The one-night with breakfast and no questions asked kind."

Annabel's eyes opened.

"Is that all they are?"

Bernadette laughed.

"Now don't bounce to the opposite extreme and get snobbish. It isn't what your parents do that matters; it's what you do."

Annabel thought of George and Ethel. She remembered with a rush of warmth how much care had been taken over her upbringing.

"It must make a difference what they bring you up like." There was all her affection for her home in her voice.

Bernadette's face contracted as if with a sudden pain. She caught her breath. She spoke almost as though she were stifling a sob.

"My God, that's true." She turned to the door as if she could not bear another moment of the discussion. "Clean up the old face; I'll go and see Miss Petoff."

Annabel looked at the shut door with a puzzled frown. Who was Bernadette? She might laugh and say that they were all the same, but she was not. Nobody at Bertna's knew anything about her. She lived in a flatlet in Bloomsbury. She was fond of reading. She spoke French, German and Italian, and had once admitted she could ride. Beyond that, nothing. No one had ever heard her mention a relation, her childhood, her school. She seemed to have drifted into Bertna's as though she had just been born. There could not be anybody with so little past.

In Tania's office Bernadette was sitting on the desk.

"She's a nice little thing. She'll be all right. Those dear creatures, Freda and Elizabeth, are making her life a burden. Come and see the kid parade. Put her out of her misery."

Tania fiddled with the papers on her desk.

"Do you think it's a mistake to take girls from comparatively humble surroundings and put them into frocks they can never afford to buy?"

Bernadette laughed.

"It's never a mistake to teach anybody to expect the best of life. Why shouldn't they have it?"

"I'm so afraid I'm teaching them extravagance."

Bernadette slid off the desk.

"You can't teach any woman that nothing but the best is good enough for her; she always knew it. All you're teaching us is to realise we can't live without it. Very immoral, I expect. Come on."

Tania got up, Bertna's would have been surprised at the familiar way their aloof Miss Petoff slipped her arm through Bernadette's.

"If I pass the child will you keep an eye on her? Freda and Elizabeth are excellent models for clothes, but not I think for little girls."

"All right, head-Nannie. Nursemaid Bernadette reports for duty, and her first job will be to dress little Miss Annabel to go down to the drawing room."

She had got it. She was engaged. She was to start work on the Monday after Christmas. She was to earn three pounds a week. It was like a fairy tale. In her bag was Bernadette's list of what she must buy. It was written in her large definite hand-writing. Annabel opened it and considered:

One pair beige satin shoes. (Very good ones. Cheap ones mean corns.)

Very long fine stockings. (Not too sun-burn, T.P. doesn't like them. Have all your stockings marked. We are robbers when we are short of a pair.)

A small satin suspender belt. (T.P. hates garters. She says they ruin good legs.)

Step-ins. As sheer as you can buy. (Two pairs will do as a start. Lux is always with us.)

Brassiere, backless. (I like net myself but some prefer crêpe-de-Chine. For number required see directions above.)

A dressing-gown to live at Bertna's. (This garment should be chosen for comfort and wearability. If, however, a wish to out-do others should predominate vast sums can be expended. If on the other hand sense is used something of manlike cut in viyella or what-not is an intelligent buy.)

Annabel folded the paper and put it back in her bag. There had been other advice not written down. She had said, 'But I need top clothes too.' How Bernadette had flared up.

"What for? Who are the top clothes to impress? Us girls in here? Don't be silly. You wait until you want something special for a real occasion. 'Very likely there'll be a garment in the stockroom going cheap. Three pounds isn't the earth you know. Save it."

Annabel looked out of the window. Nearly home. She was glad that she had not told Mum or Dad what she might be going to get. It was fun to have a surprise for them.

Ethel was in the kitchen when Annabel opened the front door.

"That you, Annabel. Get your things off quickly. Your Dad's been in twenty minutes."

George looked round the sitting-room door.

"My word, I did beat you to-day, my girl. Had to try and do the cross-word by myself. Do you know a garment in two words, three and five, that sounds like a musical composition and an encore?"

"Now, George," Ethel came to the kitchen door, "don't you start Annabel on that puzzle until she's got her things off. Don't want my steak and kidney pie kept waiting longer than it has been."

Annabel thought a moment.

"Two-piece, Dad."

Lorna looked over the bannister.

"Annabel we're going to put up the decorations after supper."

Annabel climbed the stairs.

"I'll help. What have you got?"

Alfie came out of his bedroom.

"A new sort of paper thing. When you open it out it's got little Chinese lanterns all the way up. With your shilling I got the holly."

"Annabel. Annabel."

Annabel raised shocked eyebrows at herself.

"Listen to us talking here, and now we've woken Maudie." She went into her parents' bedroom and leant over the child's cot. "What is it, pet?"

Maudie sat up, her curls standing on end.

"Oh, Annabel, I've tried an' tried not to go to sleep because I wanted to ask you sumpt'ing."

Annabel stroked the curls.

"What is it?"

"I saw a vase for Mum to-day, but it was sixpence and I've only got fourpence."

Annabel laughed. She laid Maudie down. She opened her bag and took out two pennies, and put them under the pillow.

"There darling. They'll be safe till to-morrow. Go to sleep. Annabel has to wash for supper."

Supper was almost eaten before Annabel summed up courage to tell her news. She had not realised until she started to do it how embarrassing it would be. It would be easy enough to have told of a rise to higher paid and more responsible work in the workroom. But somehow to say she was to be a model made her feel awkward. It was rather like girls must feel who had to tell the people at home they had been chosen beauty queens. However it had to be done. She took a deep breath.

"I've changed my work at Bertna's."

George laid down his knife and fork.

"Changed it! What to?"

"I'm to be a model girl. I begin the work after Christmas. I'm to be paid three pounds a week."

"A model!" Ethel looked puzzled. Then enlightenment came to her. "You mean a mannequin?"

"Yes. That's one name for them. Bertna's call them models."

"Three pounds a week." George whistled. "That's good going. What is the work exactly?"

"We wear the clothes so the customers can see how they look."

"Fat chance of their buying them after they've seen them on you," said Lorna.

Ethel frowned.

"Be quiet, Lorna. That's no way to speak." She turned to Annabel. "What made them choose you dear?"

Alfie stared at his sister.

"I thought mannequins were sort of actresses."

"I should hope not," George broke in. "Actresses indeed! We don't want anything of that sort."

Annabel looked round at them all. At their puzzled faces. Ethel tried to explain their wonder.

"Three pounds is such a lot."

Lorna had her head on one side and was studying her sister.

"I've got it. Annabel has the looks. At least she would have dressed up." She sighed. "I wish I was you. Fancy doing that all day while I go to school. Are you pleased?"

Annabel thought of those fearful unknown creatures 'the customers' before whom she would have to show. Of the long tiring fittings. Of Elizabeth and Freda. Then she thought of the cosiness of the models' room, of the friendship of a girl like Bernadette. Of three pounds a week.

"Of course I am." She smiled at her mother. "A pound a week now for you towards the housekeeping. And as for your curtain box!" She got up. "Come on you two let's fetch those decorations."

As the children ran upstairs, George shook his head.

"I don't like it."

Ethel began to pile the dishes on to her tray.

"Don't like what?"

"This new job of Annabel's. Makes me worried. She's such a good girl we don't want her growing away from us."

Ethel put down her tray. She laid her face on his hair.

"Funny old fusspot aren't you? Don't you have any faith? Girls like our Annabel don't change just because a dressmaker dolls them up in a few clothes."

George did not answer. Instead he took out his pipe and filled it. From the street came a shuffle of feet. Then under the windows some children sang.

"God rest you merry gentlemen

Let nothing you dismay."

Ethel patted his hand and went back to her work.

"There you are. Even the carol singers agree with me."

"Annabel, show this."

Annabel pulled off her dressing-gown and took the crimson evening dress off its hanger.

Bernadette looked up sympathetically from her book.

"Bad luck. Half-past five. Hope whoever it is doesn't keep you."

The door was flung open. Freda swirled in and unfastened a royal blue tulle frock.

"Off you go, Annabel. That lady dog is waiting." She turned to the other two. "It's that sweet thing The Honourable Octavia Glaye. Miss Petoff told me to show as she is so difficult and Annabel is inexperienced, but her ladyship says—" Freda put on an affected drawl. "What's the good of showing me clothes on this peroxided girl!" She changed back to her ordinary voice. "Me, peroxide! I like that. Everybody knows I'm a natural platinum."

"As natural as artificial pearls." Bernadette patted Annabel's behind. "Run along duckie, and whatever she says don't let her know you care."

Annabel had not shown sufficiently often to have got over her nervousness, but she had learnt to hide it. She paused outside the showroom door, took a deep breath and sailed in.

On the sofa at the far end Tania sat with a girl. To say that Octavia was lovely was to be hopelessly inadequate. Her beauty was breath-catching, whatever you might think of Octavia, it was as much a treat to look at her as to look at a sunset. Her cheeks had the olive tint of a peach. Old Lord Belt, her great-grandfather, had married a Spaniard, and the blood had been cropping up with success (as regards looks) ever since. Octavia had smooth hair the colour of Annabel's and large dark eyes. She was a modernised version of a primitive painting of the Madonna. To look as much like a Madonna as Octavia looked, and to be what Octavia was, presented a most stimulating mixture.

Beside Octavia sat a man. Annabel, spell-bound by Octavia's face, scarcely glanced at her companion.

"Well really," Octavia drawled. "I can't tell whether the dress is bearable or not on that girl. It's the colour I want. But it's impossible to see if the line's any good on someone who slouches round like that."

Tania looked critically at Annabel. She was not slouching. She did not show well yet, but she was not doing badly.

"Annabel is new," she whispered.

"What do you think, David?" Octavia turned to the man. "Would I look a hag in it?"

David paused to light a cigarette before he answered. Then said clearly:

"If you look half as nice in it as she does, my sweet, you'll look ravishing."

Startled, Annabel stood still and stared at the speaker. She did not see him very distinctly. Amused grey eyes, light brown hair. A curious smile as if he was looking down into a rock pool and seeing marvels. But what he was looking at was Annabel. Tania called her back to her work.

"That will do, Annabel. Put on the yellow."

Chapter Three

ANNABEL was puzzled at herself. She felt as if she had been blundering along a dark tunnel and suddenly come out into a blaze of sunlight. Not that her childhood had been dark or tunnel-like, or at least she had never thought so before. She had been perfectly happy in a quiet way. She had liked her school, and been pleased when she won a scholarship. She adored her home and was glad that her tastes lay in secure work such as Bertna's offered, and not in one of the gayer but rather come-and-go professions. She had thought all her life would be like that; quiet, uneventful, and that she wanted it that way. Essentially honest with herself she faced what was causing this upheaval in her outlook, and yet had sufficient belief in her own good sense to feel that she could not be such a fool. She, Annabel, sensible daughter of George and Ethel Brown, to be thrown into a topsy-turvy world, where you could not be sure if you were asleep or awake, where you staggered through your days as if the sun were in your eyes; just because a man looked at you as if you were a fairy tale come true.

Of course Annabel had found out who the man was. She had asked the moment she reached the models' room.

"Who is the man with the Honourable Octavia Glaye?" Bernadette was fastening the yellow frock.

"Honourables, my sweet, are titles seen but not heard. On paper they show a close connection with the peerage. In speaking they come down to plain 'Miss' like you and me." She looked at Freda. "Who is he?"

"Who do you think? Lord David de Bett of course. The papers have been hinting at an engagement for weeks."

"If all I hear about her debts is right," said Elizabeth, "I should think she'll marry him soon. He's as rich as Rothschild."

Annabel fidgeted with her frock.

"Does he want to marry her?"

Freda gave a laugh.

"People like our dear Octavia don't care whether men want to marry them or not. They just see something they fancy and suck it in."

Bernadette fixed the last hook.

"There you are. Hop along. She ought to buy."

Annabel hopped. But when she reached the showroom it was empty. It was then she had her first hint of what had happened to her. The empty showroom hurt. She was acutely disappointed. One of the showroom girls saw her and said something about Miss Glaye having forgotten an appointment and having to leave in a hurry.

"Gone!" Annabel repeated stupidly.

"That's right," agreed the girl briskly, "thank goodness too. You don't want to be kept late, I suppose?"

"No, I suppose not."

But Annabel hurrying back to the models' room had supposed nothing of the sort. Just to see that face again she would have stayed till midnight and thought every moment well spent.

Bertna's sprang into furious activity. From last year Annabel knew something of the rush attached to a dress-show. In the work-room it had been a case of Miss Bell in a permanent nervous frenzy, and the workers stitching so hard that they had no time for conversation. Downstairs in the models' room it was a matter of fittings and fittings and more fittings. Tania had designed over a hundred new clothes, which meant that each of the girls had to show about twenty-seven models. Every model needed not only endless fittings but great discussions went on during them—

Would leather buttons be smarter than cloth. Would that sash look better an eighth of an inch wider. There was something not quite right about that neck line. What was it? Then there were feuds between the women fitters and the man cutter, between the cutter and the furrier and between everybody and the woman who designed the hats. During these arguments the girls, dressed in the half finished garments, stood and let the storm blow over them. They stood upright, because someone was sure to get hysterical if they drooped. They stood stiffly because pins were wait-ing to stab at the first careless move. They wore high heels because the dresses would hang wrong if not. They were dazed with tiredness half the time, and hardly heard, and certainly did not care what alterations were made in the clothes or by whom.

Tania did what she could to mitigate the models' lot. She provided port at eleven each morning. She sent in large and indigestible buns for their tea. She made a rule that every girl was to have ten minutes' rest between fittings.

"No one who hasn't done it," she said to Miss Bell, who sniffed at the port, "knows what it is like to stand for hours on end. I can't do much to help, but what I can do I will."

Annabel was unused to standing and found it very difficult to get accustomed to. She fainted on one occasion, and
had to be allowed to rest several times. She was ashamed of
such weakness, and tried to strengthen herself with strong
mental advice.

"Pull yourself together. Don't think the room's going
round. It's mostly imagination. Everybody's tired; you aren't
the only one."

Because she was obviously fighting the fitters were kind,
even Miss Bell. They would look up at her white face, nudge
each other, and someone would whisper, "Let the poor kid
sit a minute."

In rest intervals, riding home in the train, in bed, and in
her bath, any moment, in fact, when not too tired, Annabel
considered the subject of clothes. She needed something
smart to wear in the street. And by something smart she
did not mean a reach-me-down, but one of Bertna's models
which had now gone into stock. Tentative inquiries had
produced the fact that probably she would be allowed the
two-piece, on which she had her eye, for about five pounds.
But if she bought it she would need a bag and shoes to go
with it. In fact, all her savings would go. The savings were
her own, and she could do what she liked with them. She
might get disapproval for buying the clothes; her family and
Bernadette might think she was wasteful, but they could
not stop her. But what was going to be awkward to explain
was why, having bought expensive clothes, she was wearing them every day to go to work. On the face of it nothing
could be more stupid. A girl like her without much money
ruining her only good clothes. And what excuse could she
give? She could not say—in fact she barely admitted to
herself—that it was because of a man called David, who had

seen her just once in a crimson evening frock. She was the only person who knew that she hurried through Hanover Square to catch her bus with her head down, just in case he should spring from somewhere and see the girl of whom he said, "If you look half as nice as she does, my sweet, you'll look ravishing," wearing an old shabby coat doing its third winter, flat shoes built for comfort, not for elegance, and a hat bought because it would not mind the weather.

Annabel tried to get Bernadette to herself. She wanted her not only in order to find out who to approach about the two-piece, but also for her moral support. There was no doubt the confession to George and Ethel that she was drawing out her savings would come easier if she could say "and that nice girl I told you about said she did think I ought to buy it." She cursed herself that she had ever given George her savings-book to take charge of. But before she had become a model she had never conceived doing anything that she would not first discuss with her father and mother. It proved extraordinary difficult to get hold of Bernadette, for there was no time for gossiping in the rushed pre-show days. At last, however, late one afternoon, she was lucky. Freda and Elizabeth were in the show-room, Annabel and Bernadette being fitted. The fittings finished at the same moment. Miss Bell, with tired, dragged lines under her eyes, pulled the white brocade over Annabel's head.

"There," she sighed, "not a wrinkle. Take off the fifteenth of an inch anywhere and you won't get into it." She moved uneasily on her irritated chilblain-ridden feet. "Nice time we'll have after the show when they want to try on the dresses. Our customers have busts and behinds. Why we show the clothes on you girls, who are flat all over, beats me."

The other fitter nodded.

"Usual crop of burst seams and bad tempers, I expect. Do you remember Mrs. Marks after our last? Snatched that pleated morocain Freda showed and would put it on saying it would fit like a glove. Some glove! Took four of us to get her out of it."

Miss Bell moved to the door.

"And three hours' work repairing it, and then it was never the same."

"Oh, Lord," said Bernadette as the door closed on the fitters, "am I tired?" She closed her eyes. "Do you know, except for an odd ten minutes at a time, and, of course, lunch, I've stood since nine this morning. I wish they'd never thought of trying shaded tweed. It may look spring-like, but it's taking the hell of a lot of trouble to work out. When I come to show the damn things they're hiring me a couple of setters to walk with me, and I shall need them. It's nothing but those dogs that will hold me up."

Annabel made an agreeing grunt. Then she sat up.

"Bernadette, you know that blue two-piece with the scarlet on it, in the stock-room? I want to buy it. Who do I go to?"

Bernadette opened her eyes.

"What for do you want it?"

Annabel took a deep breath.

"Well, you see, I am expecting to want something to wear, and then the thing I wear to the office is worn out, and then I have a—well, I might have to go to a wedding."

Bernadette closed her eyes again.

"I don't care why you want the wretched thing, but I do detest being lied to. You go to Miss Gale, and don't let her sting you more than a fiver. There's a hat that goes with it. If you put your foot on it and make it look like a dog's dinner, they may forget it's all right really and throw it in."

Annabel flushed. Her eyes filled with tears.

"I'm sorry," she gulped. "You've been so awfully kind I don't want to lie, but the truth is there is no reason why I've got to have it, except that I've got to."

Bernadette still kept her eyes closed, but she smiled.

"That's more like it." There was a long silence. Then suddenly she said: "Being in love isn't much fun, is it? I don't know why anybody said it was."

"Oh, but I'm not. I mean why should I be?"

Bernadette gave her shoulders a faint shrug.

"I've yet to find anybody who couldn't find a reason. Old women, middle-aged women, they all do it. Then how about us? We are at the susceptible age. It's like measles— it's something you're bound to catch." She sighed. "And catch badly and so idiotically."

"Idiotically!" Annabel found herself swept by a wave of revulsion. People said all sorts of things about love—horrid things, cheap things—and now Bernadette was saying that to love a lot was idiotic. But it was not. She felt shy and terribly young, but she could not let the expression pass.

"Loving somebody could never be idiotic."

Bernadette raised a cynical eyebrow.

"My poor sweet, I'm afraid it can."

"No." In the urgency of what she wanted to say Annabel forgot to be shy. "Of course you can be idiotic yourself. I mean people can do silly things like falling in love with a person they've never spoken to, who doesn't know they exist. But that doesn't make loving idiotic."

"I should have thought it was very near it."

Annabel clasped her knees.

"No. Just loving is worth while in itself, even if there's no love coming back." She stopped and flushed, amazed to find herself pouring out her secret thoughts. Her voice softened and warmed. "Haven't you noticed the difference it makes? You feel quite different. New all through."

Bernadette smiled.

"And the new you needs new clothes?"

"Yes." Annabel fought desperately to make her meaning clear. "You see, when I came into the model-room I was just like I was when I was at school. I never thought about myself. Now I do. I know everything about me's wrong and I want to put it right."

"For somebody you've never spoken to?"

"Yes. I suppose it does sound silly."

Bernadette did not answer for a moment. She rolled over on to her side. When she looked up the eyes she fixed on Annabel were affectionate.

"Have you ever been at a stuffy cocktail party and come out to find a lovely night, with a breeze to blow the drinks and cigarettes away?"

"No. Why?"

"That's how you've made me feel." Annabel looked puzzled. Bernadette blew her a kiss. "You wouldn't understand, duckie, so I shouldn't try."

Annabel asked for her paying-in book that evening. The supper was cleared away. George had a gardening catalogue on the table. He and Alfie were poring over it. Ethel had her chair drawn up to the fire, and though she had an enormous pile of mending to get through, she was not so engrossed that she was not free to offer advice. Lorna was at the other end of the table painting programmes for a concert she and her friends were getting up. Annabel curled up in the chair opposite her mother, looked at them all in drowsy contentment. Very engrossed they looked; it was a comfort in a way. Automatically it put off her talk with Dad. No good trying to talk about post office savings accounts when the garden was under discussion.

"Oh, Dad," Alfie begged, "couldn't we have some of those rose trees?"

George pursed up his lips. The garden was twenty foot by fourteen. At the end there was a garden fence covered with a crimson rambler. In the bed at the bottom there was a laburnum and a lilac. There was a grass plot with a gnome and a stone rabbit sitting on it. There was not a great deal of space left, but it was enough for two flower beds. Two flower beds in so small a space show very clearly. George made a point of weighing carefully the show value of every plant he put in. He shook his head over the rose tree.

"No, son. I like a rose; nothing I'm fonder of. But our beds are herbaceous. I've a fancy this year for making a show of lilies. What do you say, Mother?"

Ethel laid down the sock she was darning. Her eyes grew hazy. She was seeing a hot June evening and she and George watering a riot of Madonna lilies.

Lorna looked up from her painting.

"Let's hope there's a few deaths round here, then. Pity to grow lilies and not have a funeral."

George opened his mouth to speak, but before he had a chance Ethel said cheerfully:

"I've seen many a bride carry lilies." She looked across at Annabel. "Maybe that's what we'll need them for."

Annabel started and flushed.

"Goodness, Mum, what made you say that?"

Ethel was surprised. Jokes about weddings, and Annabel's in particular, since she was the only one of an age, were always good for a family laugh. How they had roared on Christmas Day when she got not only the ring, but a couple of china babies out of the pudding. Could she have met anyone? It was not likely; she certainly was not seeing anybody after work. She was late, of course, with that dress parade they were having, but not late enough to cover her meeting a man. Not that Ethel minded Annabel meeting a man, but she did hope that when she did it was some nice young fellow who lived round about, who could drop in and be one of the family.

None of these thoughts showed in Ethel's face. Even to Annabel's self-conscious eye she appeared only to be darning hard and listening to George. Thankfully Annabel relaxed back in her chair. What luck Mum hadn't heard what she said. Stupid of her to take her up that way. Just as if Mum wasn't always making jokes about marriage. If she had noticed the way she had flushed up, whatever would she have thought?

George licked his pencil. He began writing a list.

"We'll get them at Woolworth's this Saturday. Twelve lilies. That's the big outlay, cost all of six shillings."

Twelve lilies! Ethel saw the garden of Madonna lilies fade. Poor George; twelve would hardly give the show she wanted. She glanced up at her curtain box and mentally nodded. Easy put one or two more in when he was at work. Maybe he'd think the bulbs had come up double.

George was writing hard.

"Then we'll make up to the ten bob with tobacco plants, phlox, snapdragons, lobelias, and larkspurs if cheap—"

"And a nice packet of nasturtiums," Ethel put in. "Nothing like a packet of them for show."

George sighed. Every year Ethel wanted nasturtiums. Not for worlds would he had deprived her of them if she wanted them, but he wished she fancied something else. To his eye nasturtiums flaunting and rioting over the beds spoilt the effect at which he aimed. Stubborn growers, too; no matter what died, the nasturtiums never failed. But he showed nothing of what he felt. He merely said:

"And nasturtiums," and added the name to his paper.

Alfie studied the list with approval.

"We'll plant them on Sunday after church."

"If fine," Ethel put in. "Don't want you catching a chill, young man."

Lorna held her painting away from her the better to study it.

"I shan't garden on Sunday. It will mess up my hands. I don't want that before my concert."

George looked at her with a gleam in his eye.

"Earth never messed anyone up yet. Do you more good to spend the afternoon gardening than hanging about the streets."

Ethel looked up at the clock.

"Alfie and Lorna. Bed." She smiled at George. "The garden isn't that big we can all dig at once. Maudie is sure to want to help. Then I can't have a summer border planted that I haven't had a hand in."

"And there's me," Alfie pointed out.

"And you, if fine." Ethel looked at Lorna. "Put your things away, dearie. It's not only your hands you'll need looking nice for your concert; there's your face. You must get your beauty sleep."

Annabel stirred out of her torpor. A quick stab went through her, just between the top ribs. It was as though someone had given her a squeeze. Alfie and Lorna were going to bed. That meant she had got to ask for that book. What a fool she was to mind. She looked wistfully at Lorna, who came to kiss her good night. Such a short time ago she had been like her without a thing to hide from Mum and Dad. Why couldn't one go on being like that for ever?

George shook his head as the door shut behind the children.

"I wish Lorna had more sense."

Ethel studied her darn.

"Sense was never put into a head by grumbling." She smiled at Annabel. "Tired, dearie? If I find an old pair of gloves maybe you'd like to help in the garden on Sunday. Do you good to get some air."

Annabel nodded a vague agreement. She got up as if going to bed, then turned as if she had forgotten something.

"Oh, by the way, Dad, I want my post office book."

George nodded.

"Started paying in again? There's a good girl."

Annabel would have loved to say "Yes." For one cowardly moment she nearly did, but it was only for a moment. Lying to her father was unthinkable.

"No. I'm drawing out."

"Drawing out!" George looked at her inquiringly. "Don't like you to have to do that. With what you are earning you ought to be getting a nice bit put away."

"Not yet she can't, George," Ethel interrupted.

"It's taken her every penny she's earned to buy the under things and shoes she needed for her work. I told you we'd lent her a bit and she was only able to pay back the last of it this week. Why, the shoes alone cost twenty-five shillings, and you're not through with all you need yet, are you, dear? Is that what you want to draw out for?"

Annabel came to the table and fidgeted with her father's pencil.

"No. I can get those week by week. I'm wanting something smart for the street."

"For the street!" George looked at her in frank amazement. There were various looks Annabel could have stood, but amazement was not one of them. It made her feel the ocean that lay between her home and the man for whom she was going to dress. It made her feel what a silly little fool she was to take his light words seriously. She belonged to a world where to spend your savings riotously on a smart outfit was without precedent. He belonged to a world where girls were well dressed as a matter of course. But to know yourself a fool makes you suddenly blindly angry. Annabel turned on George.

"And why not? Why should I go on looking dowdy so no one would look twice at me? I've got the looks, though you don't seem to know it. Why should some girls have everything and me nothing? I'll spend my money how I like."

There was a pause, in which all three of them heard the clock tick. Usually its ticks were a friendly part of the house noises. In this silence they became angry knocks on a door. George got up. He went to his desk and unlocked the top drawer. He picked out the family's post office books: He selected Annabel's and handled it to her without a word.

It was one of those odd turning points that crop up in every family life. Had George been able to say the wise and understanding thing, or Annabel to have flung her arms round his neck, the quarrel might have melted in warmth. But George was essentially a family man. He loved his children round him. He loved their dependence on him. Now that Annabel was dependent no longer, he clung to small signs of authority. Sitting up to let her in on the few occasions she was late. Not for worlds would he have given her the front-door key. Expecting and, up till now, knowing all she did. Keeping her post office book. In her outburst she had not only shown how frail was the bond by which he held her, but she was taking from him one of the few holds he had. He was cut to the heart, and incapable of thinking of anything but his own hurt.

Annabel, her burst of temper over, was bitterly ashamed. She could see she had hurt George and loathed herself for it. But what could she do? She was sorry, yes. But saying she was sorry would not be enough. She must sit down and discuss with him every detail of what she would buy and why. She couldn't. She wouldn't. Her silly secret must be her own. She took the book and with a sob ran out of the room.

Ethel had never stopped darning. With each stitch she had stitched her tongue, so that it should not speak. This was between Annabel and George. Stupid to interfere. Annabel might have got a silly mood on in consequence of her new job, but she'd be better to work out of it alone. George, funny, interfering old dear, must learn sooner or later that children grew up and went their own way, even if it was a stupid way. Ethel shivered. It was as if a goose had walked over her grave. She folded her work.

"Well, old dear, what about bed?"

George had his head in his hands. He raised a ravaged face.

"You heard what she said. 'Honour your father and mother—' I've always taught them that."

Ethel laughed.

"Even the catechism doesn't say ask your father every time you want a new dress."

"It's not that." George fumbled for the right words. "She's always been my girl. All our fun. Running to catch the same train. I told you this job would make her grow away from us."

Ethel put her work-basket on the shelf. Then she drew up a chair and sat down at the table. She laid her hand on one of his.

"I was thinking of when Annabel was coming. You said to me, 'Ethel, I'm not sure I want a baby. It'll take you away from me.'"

George looked puzzled.

"What's that to do with it?"

She patted the hand under her fingers.

"Just that one day it'll be just you and me again. They'll all go, even baby Maudie. Don't forget when the time comes we were happy by ourselves."

George shook his head.

"It's different now. We've had them."

Ethel got up.

"Of course. And all this talk of Annabel's doesn't mean she's going yet, not by a long chalk. All the same, they will go and go the quicker for interference."

She held out a hand to pull George up. "Come on, wind the clock. Time we went up to bed."

George picked up the clock key. He began to wind. Then he stopped.

"But she's young. Don't want her gallivanting about in a lot of finery she can't afford, meeting we don't know who."

Ethel knelt down on the hearthrug and with the tongs took those coals off the fire which were not yet burnt through and piled them under the grate, ready for the morning. Then she looked up at George with a twinkle.

"It beats me how you can have lived with me for close on nineteen years and not rumbled me yet. Of course I'm not going to let Annabel get into a mess. Is it likely? Come on, you old silly."

CHAPTER FOUR

ON THE day of the dress show the models did not have to be at Bertna's until twelve. They were allowed to arrive at that hour in order that their hair and nails might be attended to. This time allowance caused fury in the hearts of the showroom staff. Had they not got to look especially nice that afternoon, too? Had they not got an equally tiring time ahead of them? Had they not got to stand for hours with their eyes spinning like tops in order to try and see all their pet customers at once? How, if they did not stand with revolving eyes, were they to achieve those valuable pencil scribbles? "Lady M. interested in the black ciré." "Mrs. B. wants to try on striped tailleur afterwards." "Lady F. bringing grand-daughter to see the white net."

Tania, wandering amongst the gold chairs, casting her eye over each small table to see it was properly equipped with ash-trays and cigarettes, stepping outside to see that the caterers really were bringing the necessities for tea and cocktail making, sensed a feeling of irritation. Days of dress shows might be appallingly tiring, but as a rule they were popular. What had caused umbrage this time? Then she remembered the morning off for the models. She called Miss Gale.

"Have two bottles of champagne opened."

"Who's to drink it?"

Tania laughed. She knew her faithful Miss Gale liked to feel there were some bottles of champagne to be got at in case of an emergency. She knew, too, that by an emergency Miss Gale meant something happening to herself.

"The showroom staff, including yourself. Don't look so distressed; that'll still leave four bottles. Besides, I'm not penniless, thank God. I could buy some more if I wanted it."

Tania drank a glass of champagne with the staff. In the course of swallowing it and discussing the coming show, she said:

"I hate to have you all here this morning, when you have so tiring a day ahead of you. Do rest when you have a chance. I'd have let you off, but I couldn't spare you."

When she went back to her own office the showroom said, "Isn't she sweet?" or its equivalent, which was exactly what Tania intended.

Freda and Bernadette reached the models' room first. Elizabeth came in soon afterwards.

"Did you happen to look in the showroom?" Freda asked her.

Elizabeth took off her hat carefully so as not to disarrange her curls. She scowled.

"And it was champagne."

"Don't we know?" Freda agreed.

"And us," said Elizabeth, "with more work than anybody, offered nothing. Not even a glass of port. I shouldn't wonder if I felt too bad to show this afternoon."

Freda nodded.

"Same here."

Bernadette took off her frock.

"If you do, dears, little Bernadette will revive you with bromo seltzer. It's revived your corpses before, and I dare say it will again."

Freda pulled on her dressing-gown savagely.

"It's the injustice gets me. Here are we—"

She broke off and stood open-mouthed.

Annabel had chosen the day of the dress show for the first wearing of her new clothes. The day was chosen because of the excuse it made to leave the house in them. How was Ethel (who had never been to a dress show in her life) to know they were not occasions for best clothes?

In spite of all the lovely things she had worn at Bertna's, Annabel discovered when she put on the two-piece that morning that she felt as she had never felt before. The whole of her dressing had been a pleasure. The extra time allowed made it possible for her to catch a later train. It was cold in her bedroom, but somehow the feel of nice things was warming. The small pink satin suspender belt. The sheer triple ninon step-ins, cut on the cross, so that they fitted like a glove. The net backless brassiere. A pair of her working stockings, so sheer and so bronzed. The new smart well-fitting suede shoes. Then, best moment of all, the two-piece. It was a ridiculously simple but enchantingly well-cut garment, lightened by a scrap of red on one pocket and a tiny red bow on the left breast. The hat (that had looked so deplorable when Bernadette had done with it that she had been given it for nothing) looked so different now. She put it on and got quite a shock. She had, of course, put it on before, but this morning it certainly did make her surprised at how nice she could look. The coat, so big and warm really, but managing cleverly to suggest that spring, if not in sight, was frisking just round the corner. The gloves.

The bag. At sight of the whole of herself in the mirror she caught her breath so quickly it became a hiccough, at the end of which she gasped, "And it all belongs to me."

A woman does not need to lift her eyes to know when people are admiring her. Annabel in the train, in the bus, in the street, had felt warmed by looks. The hairdresser had gone much farther than looks and had said a little wistfully (for he had a plain wife and four plain daughters), "It is wonderful to have beauty." And the manicurist had sighed and said, "I wish I was you. Must be fun being a mannequin." Annabel until such a short while ago had never thought about being envied. To be envied is a very inspiring sensation. So it was with starry eyes that she turned into Bertna's and ran up to the models' room.

Elizabeth was the first to get her breath. She put on a very refined accent.

"If you have come to see the models, modom, the show is not until three."

Freda walked slowly round Annabel.

"The blue two-piece, a fiver. That hat five and six. Shoes, bag and gloves another three pounds." She raised expressive eyebrows to Elizabeth. "All done by kindness!"

The glory of the day dropped off Annabel. Its going seemed a tangible thing, like discarding a vest. She could almost see it lying crumpled at her feet. She did not look nice; she just looked silly and dressed up. And what was she dressing up for? All the morning she had forgotten the reason for her clothes, in the pleasure of having them at all. Now it came back at her and hit her. If only she could look Freda and Elizabeth in the eyes and say, "I've spent my savings on this get-up because I'm going out to dinner with a very nice man." But she could not. Instead she crossed sadly to her cupboard, took off her coat and said nothing.

Bernadette nodded affectionately at Elizabeth and Freda.

"*There!* I hope you two little dears are feeling splendid. That was better than a glass of champagne wasn't it? Incidentally, both of you have some very nice clothes. Any reason why Annabel and I shouldn't, too?"

Freda had flushed at the beginning of what Bernadette said. By the end a cruel gleam came into her eye.

"You certainly need them with that Rolls picking you up five nights out of six."

Bernadette said nothing for a moment. Her face was white. When she did answer she sounded casual.

"Considering the Rolls has never called for me here, it must have been a nice bit of sleuthing for you to see me get into it."

Freda tried not to look ashamed.

"I just happened to be about."

Bernadette raised her eyebrows.

"Fancy being about five nights out of six. How odd."

Freda lost her temper.

"Well, I was watching you, and I don't care who knows it. With your superior air and all the languages you speak. Who are you to put on side? You're no better than the rest of us."

Bernadette lay down in her chair. Her face twisted. It seemed as though bitterness and her sense of humour were fighting each other.

"Not better," she said gently. "You under-rate yourselves. I'm worse than the rest of you. Much worse."

There was something moving in the way she spoke. She produced an embarrassed silence. Annabel, with the spirit knocked out of her, and guiltily aware that she had caused the quarrel, scurried into her dressing-gown. Freda became suddenly clatteringly busy filling the kettle and putting it on the gas-ring. Elizabeth was the first to speak.

"Well, I take it none of us girls is going out to lunch, so I suppose we ought to be getting on with the eats. If there is one thing that will send old Bell nuts it's to find us chewing when she comes down."

Bernadette got up and tied her dressing-gown sash.

"Miss Petoff said we were all to have a glass of port before we showed. I'll go and fetch it."

As the door closed Elizabeth turned on Freda.

"What on earth did you want to say that for?"

Freda looked sulky.

"She's so stuck-up."

Elizabeth put some Bovril in a cup.

"All the same, you needn't have said it to-day. With all we've got to do, we don't want to start off with a row."

Freda opened a parcel of ham.

"I just had to. Why can't she be like the rest of us? We all know about your family's boarding-house. And about Annabel's father being at Fordwych's, and about mine being dead and Mum dealing in clothes. But who is Bernadette? She's quite different to us; she's been brought up with a lot of money; anybody can see that with half an eye. But where is it? Where are her relations? Did you ever hear of a cousin? Besides, it's my belief Bernadette Lord isn't her real name."

Elizabeth stopped stirring her Bovril.

"Why?"

"Well," Freda opened a pot of butter and spread a roll, "one day when she and I were both showing for Mrs. Mears, Mrs. Mears said to Miss Petoff, 'What's that girl's name?' and Miss Petoff said, 'Bernadette Lord'; then Mrs. Mears said, 'She reminds me of—' I couldn't hear who, because the miserable cow began to whisper."

"Fancy." Elizabeth brought her Bovril over to the table. "Perhaps she's somebody's illegitimate daughter."

Annabel, who had been trying to find the courage to break in, suddenly found it.

"I think she's very nice."

Elizabeth looked at Freda. They giggled.

"You know," said Freda into space, "if there is one thing I care about it is what our dear little Annabel thinks."

Although she had been carefully rehearsed in all her clothes, and had been told by Bernadette exactly what would happen, the dress show startled Annabel.

She knew, of course, there were a hundred and fifty little gold chairs in the showroom. She must have known really that somebody would sit on them. But it had not penetrated her imagination just how it would be. Soon after two the fitters had fussed in, followed by four girls from the workroom. The sheets were taken off the dress racks, one rack for each model. A sheet was laid down by each rack, and the models given one of the workroom girls to dress them. Thankfully Annabel saw that she had been given a new hand that she did not know. It would have been awful if Margaret or Violet or one of the other girls who used to work near her had been brought down. They would have been sure to want to talk, and could not be expected to know that she was too nervous to say a word, and they would have gone back to the workroom and said she had got stand-offish. The dresses were being shown in groups. Things for the morning, the afternoon, the evening. Bernadette was showing the country and country house versions of the town clothes. Last of all were to come the court gowns.

Annabel, with her knees knocking together, allowed herself to be buttoned into a green and yellow check frock with a ridiculous little green coat to wear over it. She saw in a kind of dream two red setters led in and tied to the table leg. She saw an apparently unmoved Bernadette go over, stroke the dogs and divide a biscuit between them. She heard in a hazy way Miss Bell muttering, "Don't forget to let them see how that belt fastens." While she added *sotto voce*, "How I'll bear these chilblains, I don't know." She felt Bernadette squeeze her arm and heard her say, "Don't be scared, my sweet. Lot of dreary women with nothing to do, that's all they are." But although she saw and heard, everything had a dream quality until Miss Gale opened the door and said, "Ready, girls? Come along, Freda."

Never in her life had Annabel been so scared. It could not only be one hundred and fifty people in there. They sounded like a thousand. She was sure to fall over, to forget all she had been taught. Miss Petoff had been so kind and she depended on the way the models showed the things to sell them. But however kind people were, and however good you wanted to be, that could not prevent you making a fool of yourself when your legs were shaking so they did not know which way to go.

The showroom doors swung open. Elizabeth, with an air of extreme hauteur combined with unruffled calm, sailed through. The doors shut and Elizabeth was flying to the models' room, undressing as she ran. The doors were opening again. Miss Gale's voice seemed to come from very far away.

"Now, Annabel."

Annabel did not grasp clearly what she was doing or who she was doing it to, until she had on her third frock. For the first frock she just felt heat and light, while her brain said, 'Don't forget the pockets. Take off the belt. When you take it off show the lining of that coat. Once more round and then go out.' The second frock she became slightly more sure of herself so that she knew she was not doing anything wrong. It was the third frock that made her understand for ever what makes a good model. She was wearing a black coat and skirt with a white satin jumper and a chic little black hat with something very new and rather ridiculous in the way of a feather in it. As she stepped into the showroom, the audience laughed. For the fragment of a second Annabel paused. *Why were they laughing? Had she got something on wrong?* Then she caught the tone of the laugh. It was not the laugh at you when something is wrong, but the laugh with you when something is right and rather charming. She remembered the feather. It was silly, but gay and springlike. She smiled. She showed that hat remembering the feather was amusing and (though she did not know it) before she left the room she had sold more than a dozen of those hats. But before she left the room she felt something quite tangible. The customers liked her. They liked seeing her in the frocks. After that, the afternoon was fun.

It was when they had reached the evening dresses that Octavia Glaye arrived. She arrived just as Freda was showing the best dress she had to wear. A lovely dress in Madonna blue. Freda (who was a born model) knew that she held the audience enthralled, that she had the longing eyes of every woman in the room. She could almost feel their fingers moving towards their pencils to put a tick against that dress. Then suddenly nobody was looking at her at all. The blue dress might have been made of sackcloth for all anybody cared. Octavia had arrived.

Octavia spent five hundred a year on a publicity man. She had been a lovely much photographed baby. Later she was a much photographed child bridesmaid, and no Christmas passed but what she got into the illustrateds in fancy dress or appearing at a dancing matinée. Even her schooldays (including the awkward early 'teens) had not been allowed to pass in total oblivion. There were still bridesmaids, and when all else failed she was in the front row of house party groups, or 'caught by the camera,' bathing at Frinton. But it was not till she reached seventeen and was about to be presented that her full publicity worth was realised. Lady Harth, Octavia's mother, was an Australian with vast monies coming to her yearly from obliging sheep. She liked being Lady Harth and she liked owning Harth Castle, but she thought the English nobility backward in some things and publicity was one of them. What she argued was the good of having given birth to the loveliest debutante of the year, if the man in the street did not hear about it. Lord Harth thought publicity vulgar and regretted Octavia got such a lot of it. He never knew about the publicity man and his five hundred a year. Of course you can't have the sort of publicity Octavia had been having for three years and not feel everybody is excited every time they see you. That was why she was bound to make entrances and how she came to spoil the showing of Freda's blue frock. Freda panting into another dress gave a vitriolic description of what had happened to the models' room. Elizabeth was showing and Bernadette and Annabel too busy changing to attend properly, but the girls from the workroom enjoyed every word.

"She came in at the door and stood right in the middle of it and said in that awful affected voice of hers, 'Tania my sweet, I'm viciously late.' Of course Miss Petoff tried to shush her, but could she? No. She looked round at everybody and started waving and kissing her hand saying 'Hullo, Poppy.' 'Oh fancy seeing you here.' 'How are you darling how's your poor inside now they've cut it all out?"

"What did you do?" asked Bernadette.

"Me, I swept down to her and I said, 'Excuse me' and gave her such a look."

Bernadette ran out of the room.

"Let's hope she's found a seat by the time I get there."

Elizabeth who dashed in two minutes later had the same story to tell.

"Did that she devil Octavia make a row while you were showing, Freda?" Freda had her head in her dress and could not answer, but the workroom girl who was dressing her looked expressive so Elizabeth went on. "Spent the whole time I was showing fussing about her seat, whether she'd missed anything good, and I don't know what all. And everybody straining to look at her and whispering to each other about her and I bet they'd some pretty foul things to say. Cat! And this silver dress is so good."

Octavia Glaye was here. Annabel in a primrose faille frock waited trembling with eagerness for Bernadette to leave the showroom. Was she alone? Neither Freda nor Elizabeth had said and of course she could not ask. She clasped her hands. "Oh God do let him have come too."

Bernadette in a trailing country house frock of flowered chiffon sailed expertly and exquisitely through the doors. As they closed she gave a friendly nod to Annabel.

"The Glaye has settled down. Not that I'd care by now what she does. I can only think of my back and my feet."

The doors divided again. Annabel passed through them.

Octavia had settled into her chair. On the whole she was quite pleased. There was no doubt her arrival had caused a suitable flutter. More important still she had collected David de Bett. It was a minor triumph to have got him along. Of course everybody was whispering about them and connecting their names, but she was not deluded. She knew he was attracted, that being with her excited him. But having a man bemused and thrown into jitters by you was a very long way from having him propose. And propose he had got to. Those wretched sheep in Australia were on strike or something. At least they were either growing less wool, or it was selling for less. The Harth income was down. Octavia's father had accepted the drop and was trying to save. But Octavia and her mother had decided to gamble. Neither of them had any idea what their debts were because they would not scare themselves by adding them up. Neither of them mentioned it, but they both knew that there was a nasty day of reckoning coming if Octavia did not marry soon. Both knew that the unending credit Octavia could command was based on the belief she would marry David. So it was with the satisfactory feeling of a foot more securely on a ladder that she saw David in the seat beside her. She watched Bernadette go out of the room with a bored eye.

"I suppose they've got to make those sort of things for people who have deadly clothes to stay in other people's deadly houses. But why bore us showing them?"

David smiled.

"No good making entirely for people like you. After all there are less divine shapes."

Octavia wriggled contentedly.

"Aren't you sweet." She saw the doors re-opening and glanced at her programme to see what was coming. 'Number 48. Spring Song.' "Damn silly name for a dress—" She broke off and turned to stare at David. His chair was so close to hers they were touching. He had made a sudden movement and drawn in his breath. She followed his eyes.

Tania was clever at lighting her show. She kept the lighting round the edges of the room dim, concentrating on a soft glow on the floor space, on which her girls would walk. And since the first effect of a frock was important, she had a specially arranged light to flood down on the models as they first entered the room. It was in this pool of light that Annabel stood. David was not the only person in the room to catch his breath. Such slenderness and youthfulness ridiculously buried in such bouffant yellow skirts.

"Spring Song," said David softly. "When I was a kid that was just how I imagined spring would look."

"Did you!" Octavia tore a corner off her programme. "I never think spring is gawky. That girl's all hands and elbows."

David looked at her and laughed.

"With your looks you can afford to be generous. Of course she hasn't your poise, why should she have. But she has simplicity."

Annabel walked slowly, her eyes raking the chairs. Was he there? Then suddenly she saw him. The same amused grey eyes, with a warming look of admiration at the back of them. She had to pass on; but her heart sang. "I've seen him. I've seen him. He's here."

Octavia was in a furious temper. She had not brought David to a dress show to have him making eyes at the models.

He had been very unwilling to come, well she would pretend to be unselfish. She would take him away again.

"I never saw such messy clothes," she grumbled. "Let's go."

But David shook his head.

"I, on the contrary, like the clothes. And I am certainly not going to offend Tania, whom I adore, by leaving at the end of ten minutes. Here I am and here I sits."

Octavia tried a method she had found occasionally successful with other men. She used baby talk.

"But 'ittle 'tavia's hot. Wants to go home."

David looked disgusted.

"My dear Octavia must we sink quite as low as that. I never much cared for nurseries. But nursery talk from someone of your experience is obscene."

Octavia wriggled her shoulders angrily.

"You are being hateful."

He patted her hand.

"No, darling. I adore you, but even you make mistakes. Baby talk is one."

Octavia pulled herself together, and to the room at large she gave the effect of "happy young woman escorted by admirer." Inside she was seething. "I know why he won't go" she told herself. "It's the dark mannequin. Little rat, I'll teach her."

The last of the evening dresses had been shown.

There was a pause while cocktails were handed round. The customers drank in pleasant anticipation. "The Court gowns, always a pretty sight."

Each of the models had one court dress and train. The showing of them was a carefully arranged finale. In their veils and feathers they all appeared at once. They paraded round the room. Then back at the door they formed in a line, curtsied and withdrew.

Octavia watched this performance closely. She had of course been presented and knew all there was to know about handling a train. She had curtsied on many occasions to Royalty and knew just how a curtsey should look. Her eager eye spotted in a moment that these curtsies were effective rather than correct, and that Annabel might have wobbled had she not been steadied by her next door neighbour.

The girls' curtsies and exit was followed by a round of applause. On top of it came Octavia's voice.

"Tania darling. Too divine. I wonder would it be a bother if that little dark girl came back. I'd like to have another look at that frock."

Tania nodded.

"Of course." She turned to Miss Gale. "Call Annabel."

Annabel still radiant because at least David was under the roof, was removing her feathers when the call came. She looked up startled.

"Me, Miss Gale. Why?"

Miss Gale was not accustomed to be asked "why." In any case she did not know "why." Her feet ached.

Her back ached. The show was over and it was time the customers went home.

"Because Miss Petoff says so. That's enough."

The customers were standing up to go when Annabel came in at the show room door. They paused smiling at how pretty she looked.

"Oh, here's the girl." Octavia came forward. She made a pretence of fingering Annabel's frock. Then she drew back, her head on one side. "Yes, I like it. I think it will do. Just walk up to the end of the room will you and then turn and curtsey. I want to see the line."

Turn and curtsey! Annabel's eyes goggled. Turn and curtsey! That awful court curtsey that no one had taught her properly, and she only managed by one hand on the floor or holding Bernadette. How terrifying to be made to do it alone with all those people looking. How miserable to make a fool of herself with him there.

Stiff with nerves, she moved to the end of the room, rather clumsily swung round, came back towards Octavia. Now for the curtsey. Left leg behind. Keep your back straight. She was wobbling. She was going. Annabel, amid a roar of laughter, found herself sitting on the floor. Octavia turned to Tania.

"Why on earth don't you have girls who can do a curtsey. How do I know how this dress will look with this gawk falling all over the place."

Annabel felt red from the soles of her feet to the top of her head. "This gawk." To be called that with him there listening. Her eyes filled with tears. Tania patted her shoulder.

"Annabel's new. She'll be able to curtsey soon. Run along, you've done very well."

In the passage leading to the models' room there was a cupboard. One side of it made a dark corner. Annabel crouched in to this and cried. "This gawk." Then Miss Petoff saying kind things to her as if she were a little girl in the school-room. What must he think? He'd never admire her again. Never. It was at this part in her moans that she needed a handkerchief. She looked in a dazed way at her dress as if she would suddenly find one sticking out of it. Then something caught her eye. It was a ear-ring hanging on her veil. She picked it off wonderingly. A diamond ear-ring! Whose could it be. Then suddenly she remembered it was Miss

Glaye's. It must have fallen there when she was looking at her dress.

Forgetting her tear-stained face, Annabel ran back into the showroom to look for Tania. No one was there. There were voices from the office, but she dare not go in. She looked at the ear-ring in desperation, and then had an idea. Perhaps Miss Glaye had not gone. She might catch her at the door. She hung her train over her arm and ran.

"No," said David, "you're divine, but a little cat. I won't go in your car, Octavia dear. I shall walk."

"Home," Octavia growled at her chauffeur.

The car slid out into the traffic. David looked after it with a queer smile. Then he heard a gulp at his elbow. He looked round.

"The Spring Song!"

Annabel held out the ear-ring.

"It's hers. I found it in my veil."

"Did you?" He took the ear-ring and looked at her with his head on one side. "Do you live permanently in yellow evening frocks and court gowns, or have you anything else?"

Annabel laughed shakily.

"Of course. My own clothes."

"Then go and put them on. Lovely ladies who fall over their trains need cocktails to restore them. And that's just what I'm going to take you to have."

CHAPTER FIVE

IF YOU have spent seventeen years going quietly on your way, pleased with little things, it is confusing when life gives a jolt and throws you into something big. Annabel ran up the stairs at Bertna's in a dream. It couldn't be true. Of course she had been thinking a lot about David de Bett, even buying clothes in case she met him. But it had been rather like dressing in case you met Robert Taylor or Gary Cooper, it did not mean you ever expected you would. And here she was running upstairs to put on her new two-piece to go out with the man. He was waiting in a taxi. It couldn't be true.

In the passage she met Miss Gale, who looked at her in shocked surprise.

"Annabel! What are you doing, dashing about in a presentation gown?"

Annabel gave her a vague smile.

"Somebody dropped a ear-ring. I went down to give it back."

Miss Gale made an annoyed clicking sound with her tongue against her teeth. She thought the reply most inadequate, and would have liked to have said so, but there was such an imperious air about Annabel that she felt any thing she said would be a waste of time, so she contented herself with a final "Tchah!" which might have meant anything, and went to Tania's room.

Tania, completely exhausted, was sprawled in an arm-chair. She had a cocktail in her hand and the shaker was on the floor at her feet. At the sight of Miss Gale she reached for another glass, and poured her out a drink.

"Thank God, the customers left a bit over. Lord, am I tired? But didn't we do well. Order after order, we'll be busy for weeks."

Miss Gale took her cocktail and sat primly on one of the stiffer chairs. She liked to see Tania relax, in fact, she frequently urged her to, but she never felt that relaxing was suitable to herself. She sipped her drink.

"I suppose you've never thought that new model at all queer in the head?"

Tania stared at her.

"My poor sweet, has the show upset your business sense. Didn't you realise this afternoon that Annabel was a find. They adored her."

Miss Gale lit a cigarette.

"That may be. But she had a very queer look on her face just now. Very queer."

Tania laughed.

"So have you. So have we all, if it comes to that. We're squinting with tiredness. Drink up, and don't get morbid about my models."

The models' room was in confusion. An army of people under Miss Bell staggering away with the frocks, hindered by the showroom staff, who kept appearing to say: "Don't let the rust tweed go up. Mrs. Lemon is trying it on in the morning," or "Keep the emerald and black afternoon handy, I'm expecting Mrs. Morris in about it, and she always comes early."

Elizabeth, in her knickers, brassiere, feathers and veil, was wearily removing her stockings. Bernadette was dressing slowly but steadily, regardless of the muddle around her. Freda was lying down. She still wore her court dress, but she had hung the train and most of the skirt over the back of her chair. She was eating a large bath bun and washing it down with bromo seltzer. Nobody had much energy to ask what had delayed Annabel.

"Did someone buy that dress?" Elizabeth inquired, but when Annabel shook her head, she had not the interest to bother further.

Annabel, changing as quickly as her trembling fingers would let her, was thankful for the fuss around her. Very likely nobody would notice she was in a hurry. Nobody might have if Miss Bell's attention had not suddenly been called to Freda.

"Freda! What are you doing sitting about in that gown? You know you mayn't sit in the models."

Freda lifted the skirt to show that she was not sitting on it.

"These?" She looked down in pretended surprise at her knickers. "These aren't models."

"Now, Freda, no impertinence." Miss Bell moved angrily on her tortured feet. "You're sitting on the dress, and you know it; and eating in the dress, what's more. If you don't take it off at once, I shall be bound to report you to Miss Petoff."

Freda got crossly out of her chair.

"Oh, all right. But I'm tired. You can't expect us to rush about after all we've done this afternoon." At that moment her eye fell on Annabel, who was dressed and carefully arranging her hat before the glass. "Except our dear Annabel, who we know has a date."

Annabel turned round, crimson and anxious.

"I haven't. Of course, I haven't." She picked up her bag and ran out of the room.

Freda looked at Elizabeth.

"You know, when I said that I meant it as a joke. But now I'm beginning to wonder. We must look into this."

David, sitting in his taxi, wondered what had induced him to invite Annabel for a drink. Of course, she was pretty, but he had never run after pretty shop assistants. Waiting for her, he lit a cigarette and brooded. Why had he? Then suddenly he was shocked to discover his motive. He was apologising for Octavia. Odd how that hurt him. He was in no way under any illusion about Octavia, but she enthralled him, and he wanted to love her. Sooner or later he must marry, he must have an heir. How satisfying to have a wife whom you not only loved, but who set all your pulses hammering. Octavia, at present, did the pulse hammering all right, but did he love her? Sometimes, almost. She had a recklessness and courage he found endearing. Then she did things like to-day. She, who had everything, made a fool of a little mannequin with nothing. The thought of the scene and the court dress brought him back to Annabel. Where should he take her? She did not look the sophisticated sort one met at the Embassy or Ciro's. Perhaps she would look nothing out of Tania's creations. No good deciding where to take her until he saw her. He would have liked the Berkeley Buttery, but perhaps something quieter would be better, where he wouldn't meet people he knew.

Annabel came down the steps. She looked shyly at the taxi. David glanced up and saw her. He jumped out and opened the door, giving her a quick approving look. He turned to the taxi driver.

"The Berkeley Buttery."

Annabel was disgusted to find that being alone with David tied her tongue up as if it had been knotted. David, sensing this, rattled into a monologue.

"You mustn't feel shy, Spring Song. I'm not at all the sort of person to be shy with. Here, you see the fool of the family. My dear mother was not gifted in the matter of producing sons. She had six daughters, all intelligent with a strong leaning to good works. Then, most unexpectedly, when I was despaired of, I appeared. Poor child, the doctors said. Yes, he is a boy, but a wretched specimen. His grey matter would sit on a threepenny bit. Do you know what grey matter is, Spring Song?"

Annabel, who knew perfectly, could only shake her head.

"It's brains. It took the united efforts of three governesses, one preparatory school, and four coaches to get me into Eton. As for Oxford, several strong men died pushing me into Magdalen."

Annabel, who had never had anything to do with Oxford, puzzled over this last statement. "Maudlin," surely that meant "sloppy." David grasped she had misunderstood him.

"Magdalen is one of those names like Marjoribanks or Leverson-Gower, that is set up as one of the permanent pronunciation puzzles of the British race. I think we invent them to keep the foreigner from knowing the language too well."

Annabel came sufficiently out of the lethargy into which his closeness had thrown her to make a mental note. Evidently "Maudlin," where David had been, was not spelt that way. She would find out about that, she did not want to seem ignorant. Octavia Glaye would know things like that.

David smiled at her thoughtful face.

"I don't wonder you look thoughtful. You're saying, 'and then, what?' Well, the gods having made a fool, fortunately decided he could not be expected to earn his own living, and they provided the wherewithal for him to live in worthless leisure. But they reckoned without my mother."

They were on ground at last that Annabel understood. Often had she heard Ethel on the subject of what trouble came from idleness.

"That's like my mother. She says, 'If you're busy, you're happy.'"

David grinned.

"Our mothers ought to meet. They sound two girls with but a single thought."

Annabel was eager to learn all she could about him.

"What did your mother put you to?"

"She didn't exactly put me to anything. But she tried to put me to everything, from being a Scout leader to scene-shifter-in-chief for the Women's Institute. But I was against it. There's been such a lot of good works done by my family I thought it wouldn't hurt to give them a rest. Besides, you know there's heaps to do looking after the place. I try to make it productive. It employs labour."

Annabel said nothing. His idea of "heaps to do" and hers, obviously did not synchronise. Heaps to do did not mean you were free to run about in the afternoon with people like Octavia. He caught something of what she was feeling.

"I'm in town on business really. Very family business. My mother thinks it's time I settled down."

He spoke lightly, dismissing the subject. Annabel would have liked to ask if he were engaged to Octavia, but she was sure he did not want to be questioned.

The taxi stopped at the Berkeley. He led the way through to the Buttery. They had a halting progress. He seemed to know everybody. In a confused way she heard a lot of "Hullo, David," and saw a blur of smiling faces. Then she found herself sitting in a chair, apparently made of tweed, at a black-and-gold shiny table.

David handed her his cigarette case. Annabel had never smoked, though she had often meant to try. She wondered if this would be a good moment to start, but decided against it. She had heard somewhere your first cigarette sometimes makes you sick.

"I don't smoke, thank you."

"Quite right, too." David lit one. "White man's grave." He picked up the list of drinks and pushed the almonds across to her. "What shall it be?"

Annabel had never drunk a cocktail. She had no idea what to ask for.

"I've never had one, so I don't know."

He put the card down and studied her.

"Aren't you a nice person. Would you like to start on a small one to-day? Or shall it be a tomato juice?"

Annabel considered.

"Would a little one go to my head?"

He shook his head.

"No. Not the one I shall order you. But beware of them. If you are out with fatherly men like your Uncle David, it's all right. But there are big, bad wolves disguised as men, who might enjoy giving you something too strong." He beckoned to the waiter. "An orange blossom, with just half the usual gin, and a gin and French with the extra gin left over from the orange blossom." He turned to Annabel. "Here you see a warning before you. The man who wants the extra drop." He leant forward. "You know, Spring Song, I don't know your name. I heard the Annabel bit, what else is there?"

Annabel wished she could say Montmorencey or De Haviland or something like that.

"Brown."

"Annabel Brown. Who doesn't smoke and is having her first cocktail. Where do you live, Annabel? Did you come out of an enchanted forest?"

Annabel felt a little twinge. She loved her home, but, really, after "enchanted forest," to say 110, Mercia Lane, Coulsden, sounded a bit drab. But she did not have to say it. Just as she opened her mouth, somebody laid a hand on David's shoulder, and said: "Well, if it isn't himself."

David got up.

"Hullo, Daphne. This is Miss Annabel Brown. Annabel, Miss Daphne Fare. She writes."

Annabel looked up and saw a tall, twinkling-eyed woman, with greying hair and a young face.

"How do you do," she said shyly.

"I do very nicely, thank you." Daphne turned back to David. "Can I sit down a second? I'm having a drink with my publisher, and the hound's late."

David pulled up a chair.

"How's life? Gin and French?"

Daphne nodded.

"Grand. It would be better if I didn't subsist on novels for a living. How's yours? How have you sailed past the syren's song into this pleasant harbour?"

David frowned at his cigarette.

"You're not fair to her. You never have been. You've never taken the trouble to know her."

Daphne twinkled at him.

"It would be no trouble. The character is written so clear, that she who runs can go on running while reading." She turned to Annabel. "Do you know the lovely Octavia?"

"Well, not know exactly. You see, I'm a model at Bertna's, and she buys her clothes there, so it's more knowing her by sight."

"And quite near enough." Daphne gave her an appraising look. "Have you been at Bertna's long?"

"Nearly a year really, but only a model since Christmas. I was in the workroom before."

Daphne turned to David.

"I hope you appreciate honesty when you meet it." She looked up and waved. "There's my publisher." She got up and nodded at Annabel. "He shall bring you round to have a drink. Fix a night with him. My blessings on you both."

David turned to look after her in order to give himself time to think. He had not thought of continuing this acquaintance. But there was something about Annabel that made him feel it would be nice to see more of her. It was as good as a long country walk to meet someone so unaffected.

"Well?" he asked. "What night shall it be?"

Annabel finished her drink.

"It doesn't make any difference to me. I never do anything special after I've finished."

"Don't you?" David eyed her with amusement. He knew she was totally unconscious of the interested eyes on her, or just how many people would ask him later who she was. Girls with her face did not grow on bushes. In a year, even in six months, she would probably answer the same query with: "Well, I can't manage anything for a fortnight, but I might fit it in after that." But all he said was: "Right, then I'll fix it with Daphne and let you know." He called for his bill. "How do you go home?"

"By train from Victoria."

He took her arm.

"Come along. I'll drop you at the station."

The family were at supper when Annabel came in. Ethel went into the kitchen to get her food from the oven.

"Well, you are late. Fancy it going on this long. Some people can't have anything to do, except buy clothes."

Annabel pulled out her chair. Lorna regarded her in amazement.

"Gosh! Look at you. I never saw such lovely clothes."

Alfie stared.

"You look like a film star."

George, though he did not want to argue with Annabel again, felt it was a mistake to let the younger children think clothes mattered.

"Handsome is as handsome does."

Ethel put a plate of food in front of Annabel. She kissed her cheek.

"This time it's both ways, is and does, isn't it, dearie?"

Annabel was feeling mean. She had not lied about the time she had left Bertna's. She had just not answered. All the same, not answering was lying, in a way, and she hated to do that to Mum.

"It wasn't the dress show that made me late." She filled her mouth so as not to have to explain for a bit. It was not really a good move, because it meant that all her family stopped eating and looked at her with interest. Interest when your mouth is full, and you are embarrassed anyway, has a bad effect. Annabel choked.

Alfie, who was next to her, thumped her on the back. Lorna passed her a glass of water. When, panting, with eyes full of tears, she recovered, she quite hoped that her doings might have lost interest. But George was waiting.

"If it wasn't your work kept you late, what did?"

Odd how nothing Ethel said could annoy, and most things that George said did. Annabel had to keep a hold on herself not to snap, "That's my business, isn't it?" But she was sorry for what she had said the other night. So she answered quietly:

"I went to have a cocktail."

When people do not drink cocktails there is a tendency to count all those who do as goats, while considering themselves numbered among the sheep. The Browns not only never drank cocktails but knew no one who did. George drank beer, and Ethel now and again at Christmas or on a holiday had a glass of port. The news had a tremendous effect. Alfie said:

"Cocktails! Gosh!"

Lorna, who had long lamented to her girl friends the narrowness and conventionality of her home, felt things were looking up. Her eyes shone.

"What did it taste like? Who gave it to you?"

George, trying to control himself, but shocked at the rapid way in which Annabel was moving dogwards, collected himself to speak, but Ethel was too quick for him.

"Did you, dear?" Her voice was as casual as though she made a habit of a daily cocktail herself. "Where did you go?"

Annabel licked her lips. There were places so august and renowned that everybody knew about them, even if they never expected to go into them. Now she had gone in, she had drunk an Orange Blossom in one of the most renowned of them all.

"The Berkeley Hotel." Even as she said it and saw her family's faces she knew what a joke it was. After all, the Berkeley had not been frightening at all. She had not felt out of place or looked it. But, somehow, saying "I had a cocktail at the Berkeley Hotel," was just as improbable as saying "I dropped in to tea at Buckingham Palace." She giggled.

"Annabel! The Berkeley Hotel?" Lorna screamed. "You didn't go there, you've made it all up."

Annabel was laughing so much, she could only shake her head.

Ethel was delighted with her. To go to places like that and come home all grand would not have been like her

Annabel. To come home and laugh was just what she would have done herself.

"What was it like inside?"

Annabel, with instinctive tact, turned to her father.

"Oh, Dad, there were some lovely flowers about. Sort of thing you see in the florists' and masses of them."

"I dare say. With all the money people throw away at those places they can afford it."

Ethel shook her head at him.

"Now, Dad. She's had a nice time. Don't want to spoil it all." She turned back to Annabel. "What was your cocktail called? They all have names, don't they?" She winked at George. "See what a woman of the world you married."

"It was called"—Annabel began to laugh again— "Orange Blossom."

How they screamed. It was like Christmas Day when Annabel had got the ring and the china babies out of the pudding. Even George had to laugh. Each time they stopped, one of them exploded on the words "Orange Blossom!" and off they all went again.

"Oh, well," said Ethel at last. "They say laugh and grow fat. With the laugh I've had to-night I ought to put on a couple of pounds."

Lorna leant across the table.

"Who took you to the Berkeley Hotel, Annabel?"

Annabel paused for the fraction of a second. If she gave David his title, it would sound like side. Beside, Mum and Dad would worry.

"A man called David de Bett, Miss Nosey Parker."

Ethel nodded.

"That's right, Annabel. I tell her putting her nose in to all the things she does, it'll hang down like a trunk one day."

Lorna shrugged her shoulders crossly and moved over to the window. Idly she twitched back the curtain and stared into the street. Ethel had meant to ask her to come and help clear the supper things. But to ask Lorna to help when she was upset was to have a row. She and Annabel exchanged understanding glances.

"I'd offer to help," Annabel said, "but I can't in these." She looked down at her new clothes.

"I should think you couldn't. Besides, you've done enough standing about for one day. You go and take off those new things and put on your dressing-gown, and come down and have a warm before you go to bed."

Lorna glanced over her shoulder as the door shut on Annabel. No one was looking at her, or they would have been puzzled by the bitter expression on her face. She turned back to the window, her eyes full of tears.

"'Tisn't fair," she thought. "Here's me, in my old blue and Mum won't even give me some silk stockings. If I had nice clothes and silk stockings, perhaps men would take me out. I'd look much older if I was dressed different. It's mean. It's mean."

When the children had all gone to bed and George was winding the clock, Ethel gave his back an understanding smile.

"I was pleased with Annabel."

George went on winding in silence for a moment. When he spoke his voice was deliberately gruff.

"She's all right. But I don't like these cocktails."

Upstairs, Annabel was having a bath. Luxuriously she let the hot water run over her toes. She leant back and smiled happily at the ceiling. Wasn't life exciting. She had been out with David. She had drank a cocktail. She had been to the

Berkeley. And, greatest wonder of all, she was seeing him again. She was so happy, it hurt inside.

Octavia that night went to dine at the Embassy. In the cloak-room, she ran into a woman friend called Avril.

"Hullo, Octavia. How's things?"

Octavia powdered her nose carefully. Privately, she considered she had mucked up her day. Idiotic of her to quarrel with David, and all about a silly little trollop, who mattered to nobody. Tiresome he had been out when she phoned. Lucky she was lunching with him to-morrow. She must be extra nice, and smooth things over. Of course, none of these thoughts must reach Avril, whom she considered a cat. She turned a serene, well-made-up face towards her.

"Heavenly, darling."

Avril gave a nice performance of a slightly surprised girl friend.

"Really?" She flicked a grain of powder off her chin. "Only I wondered what the boy friend was doing with the lovely unknown baby brunette in the Berkeley Buttery."

Not by a flicker of an eyelash did Octavia show how the news hurt.

"Oh, that girl! He had to take her out. A duty civility."

"Fancy." Avril collected her bag. "Aren't some men lucky. They manage to look as if they enjoyed facing their duty more than their pleasure."

The look Octavia threw at Avril's departing back would have frozen a less experienced spine. She picked up the comb and arranged an already neat curl. "Lovely unknown brunette." Now, who? She was quite certain of the answer. So he had sunk to shop girls had he? Well, she'd teach her. She'd find a way.

Octavia went back to the man with whom she was dining, with such a glint in the eye that he noticed it.

"You look very feline."

She picked up her liqueur glass and sniffed her Kümmel.

"Between you and me, not nearly as feline as I feel. Nor nearly as feline as somebody is going to find I am."

There were signs of spring in London. Crocuses pushed up through the grass in the park. There were buds on the daffodils. Everybody began to feel shabby in their winter clothes. Definitely spring clothes, gay but warm, are for the rich. But a spring look is possible to the poor. The bright scarf or new hat. Little bunches of artificial spring flowers were fashionable. Hardly a coat but had its bunch of cowslips or snowdrops. Even the charlady at Bertna's had a spray. It was mimosa. "Cost four-pence," she told a friend, "on account of the best bit bein' broke. But it puts heart in me to see it."

David did not need all these signs of stirring sap. He felt the spring as he had never known it before. The first green buds hurt. The catkins made him restless. He could not stay in one place. He was always dashing to his home in Sussex, and no sooner was he there than he had to be in London. He was cross with himself because he knew he was a fool. But he did not understand himself, and there it was. Tennyson wrote "In the spring a young man's fancy lightly turns to thoughts of love." David wondered what Tennyson would have written about the young man whose thoughts turned to two loves.

On his drives to Sussex and back he tried to clarify these thoughts. Octavia! He wanted to want to marry her. She had been brought up to do the sort of things his wife would have to do. She was lovely as a May morning. She was what his mother called "suitable." Everybody was waiting to see the engagement announced. And what was stopping it being announced? Even to himself, David only half admitted it was Annabel. What did he feel about Annabel? Something so different from what he felt about Octavia, that he told himself of course it wasn't love. He drought perhaps "brotherly" was what it was, only he could not be sure as he had never felt brotherly about his sisters. He was always wanting to look after her. He worried that she was overworked. He worried that she did not eat enough. He would wake in the night worrying in case she was ill. He never worried over Octavia, all he felt was a wish to have his arms round her. If he thought of her when she was not there, that was the way he thought about her. He knew he must get married, and Octavia was right for the job. Yet, somehow, after each meeting with Annabel the idea of marrying Octavia grew more impossible. Funny, how shoddy Annabel's simplicity made Octavia's sophistication appear.

Annabel herself was barely conscious of anything. She scarcely knew that spring was coming because every day was glorious to her whether the sun shone or whether it rained. She lived in a daze outwardly doing those things she had to do, but wrapt away from other people in her dreams. David had not gone out of her life. That first cocktail at Daphne's had not been the last. There were other meetings. Twice she had dined with him. One Sunday she had met him for lunch and they had motored into the country afterwards. When she heard a bird sing, or saw a flower it was not 'Spring' they said to her, it was 'David.'

Her preoccupation escaped notice nowhere. Tania sent for Bernadette. She passed the cigarette box.

"That kid Annabel looks in love. Do you know anything about it?"

Bernadette lit her cigarette.

"No." She gave Tania a rather lop-sided smile.

"My own troubles have filled my fore-ground lately."

"Yours!" Tania angrily tapped the ash off her cigarette into a tray. "If you had a grain of sense—"

"Or of courage." Bernadette broke in. "I wouldn't have any troubles. But I haven't so we shall never be able to prove the truth of that statement."

Tania looked at her affectionately.

"Don't let's quarrel. Besides it's not you I've got you here to talk about." She leant back and blew a smoke-ring into the air. "You remember when I took Annabel on, a conversation we had? I had my doubts if it was fair plunging her into a world to which she didn't belong."

"And you said 'if I pass her will you keep an eye on her.' Is that what you're reminding me?"

"Yes. Have you kept an eye on her?" Bernadette sat on the edge of Tania's desk.

"I've done all I can. I've kept Freda's and Elizabeth's claws out of her. I've told her what to buy in order to show clothes in your shop. And I think she likes me sufficiently to confide in me."

"Do you?" Tania picked up a slip of paper. "Did you know she had mortgaged three weeks salary to-day in order to buy clothes from the stock-room."

Bernadette opened her eyes.

"No. If she meant to do that she wouldn't tell me for she'd know I'd disapprove. What's she bought?"

"That green suit, and the blue silk and wool with the spots. And the green hat that goes with the suit."

"Quite a trousseau." Bernadette looked thoughtfully out of the window. "Well, after all, it's no good blaming yourself. She was just as likely to fall in love in the workroom."

"But not to need all those clothes. This smells to me as if she'd fallen for someone this end of the world. She'd never want all these things for some boy near home. She'd be more likely buying shorts to do something sensible like hiking."

Bernadette nodded in agreement.

"She wears her two-piece to work every day. I suppose she sees whoever it is when she finishes here."

"That's about it. And from the look of the poor little thing she's in love. Not a very safe state to be in when you believe all love ends at the altar steps."

Bernadette jumped up. She stubbed out her cigarette.

"I'm a selfish beast. She's an enchanting child. I wouldn't have her hurt for worlds. I'll keep an eye on her and try and learn which way the wind is blowing."

In the models' room Freda and Elizabeth were fingering the green suit and the blue frock with the spots. Annabel was in the showroom.

"Dear, dear." Freda nodded sadly at the clothes.

"How our little innocent has fallen. Do you know who?"

Elizabeth shook her head.

"No. I've been going somewhere every night for weeks. I've had no time to watch our Annabel."

Freda examined the green hat.

"I've an idea. Not certain. But I saw her get into a car the other night. I may be mad, but if the face I saw was the face I thought I saw there's going to be a lot of fur flying."

"Tell me."

"No." Freda went to the cupboard and mixed herself a bromo seltzer and got a chocolate biscuit.

"If I'm right about this there might be something in it."
She sipped her drink. "When there's something in anything,
little Freda likes keeping it to herself."

Ethel lay in bed. She lay on her side as still as if she
slept. She did not want to disturb George. He was too apt
to worry as it was. Say one word about what was on her
mind and he would go off the deep end. What was Annabel
doing? Late two or three times a week. So in love she could
not hear when she was spoken to. Who was this David de
Bett? Why didn't she bring him home, she had asked her
often enough. She had brought Annabel up well no doubt
of that, but if this man meant harm would the upbringing
hold? A tear rolled down her nose. She could not fumble for
a handkerchief, so she sniffed. The sniff disturbed George,
who was a light sleeper. He opened his eyes.

"What is it old girl? Anything wrong?"

Ethel reached for his hand and held it.

"Course not, silly, just a bit of a cold. You go to sleep."

A gipsy was selling primroses in Hanover Square. A *sotto
voce* barrel organ was whispering "When you grow too old
to dream." Annabel stood on the steps of Bertna's. The gipsy
stared, the organ grinder stared. Even in Hanover Square
it was not often they saw someone so pretty. The organ
grinder grinned at the gipsy.

"Looks like Spring in that green, don't she."

An angry looking racing car drew up at the bottom of
the steps. David looked out.

"Hullo poppet, I say who's got new clothes. Don't you
look lovely. Hop in."

The car moved off up the square.

Freda and Bernadette met in the passage. They had both said "Good night." Both should have gone. Bernadette grasped what had happened.

"So you've been peeping round the curtain too." Freda nodded, pleased with herself.

"My word. See who it was? That's who I thought, only I couldn't believe it. Who'd have guessed it. She looks so innocent."

"It is conceivable that she is. I've often thought you and Elizabeth took an unnecessarily low view of the male sex."

Freda gave her a nasty look.

"Where's your Rolls to-night?"

Bernadette had reached the steps into the street. She paused. The barrel organ had changed its tune.

It was now murmuring—"get weary, wearing the same shabby dress." She let the phrase finish. Then she turned to Freda.

"How sordid you make things."

Freda shrugged her shoulders.

"Don't be sloppy. I wasn't born yesterday."

Bernadette went down the steps.

"Feeling your years, dear?" Then a thought struck her. She turned and laid a hand on Freda's arm. "Nobody must know what we saw. She's a little fool to let him come here. Bound to be talk sooner or later."

Freda shook her arm free.

"Not from me there won't be. Some information's too valuable to give away. Well, so long, I've a date."

Freda's date was at Ciro's. It was with a nitwit young man in the Coldstreams, called Freddie. She liked Freddie. She thought him a fool, but he was easy to handle, she hardly had to dig to get her gold. A wistful reference to 'nothing to wear,' was almost sure to touch his over-soft heart. To-night she was particularly pleased with herself, she had a new black frock in which she looked as fair as a moonbeam. And she had the satisfaction of knowing that Freddie was not the only man to wilt at sight of her. She had another satisfaction, three tables from her, Octavia was dining with David de Bett.

"Evidently only gives Annabel a drink." Freda thought. Quite right, too, she'd not be used to places like this.

During a pleasant meal, spent in leading Freddie up and down the garden path, Freda gave thought to Octavia. It seemed like fate she should be eating in the same room with her. Surely they could not have been thrown together without purpose. Looking at the other table she succeeded in persuading herself that Octavia was a poor ill-used little thing, and she a ministering angel sent to right a great wrong.

Octavia at her table had noticed Freda, whom she knew by sight. She considered her carefully without pointing her out to David. She noticed the greedy mouth, the general air of brilliance without heart.

"She's just what I want," she thought. "Luck seeing her here."

Dinner over she shifted her chair, so that she slightly faced the other table. A minute later Freda looked up. The two girls exchanged a look. Without a word they swept up their bags and went to the cloak-room.

Octavia and Freda stood in front of the same glass powdering their noses.

"Would you like to pick up a quick fiver?" Octavia enquired.

Freda had a pleased smile. She had not thought it would be as easy as this. She had thought she might have to be the first to mention rewards.

"Yes."

"Well get the home address of that girl Annabel, who models with you, and let me know if she's expecting to be in about tea-time on Sunday?"

Freda made up her mouth.

"Shall I telephone?"

"Yes. Where shall I send the boodle?"

"Bertna's. Nobody will know."

They nodded at each other and left the room as strangers.

Octavia lay on her face on her sitting-room floor. She had a road map stretched in front of her. Suddenly she looked up. The St. Clouds had a house somewhere near Three Bridges. What could be better. She got up, found her address book and picked up the telephone receiver.

"Oh, is her Ladyship in? No, don't disturb her. Just ask whether Miss Glaye might motor Lord de Bett down to lunch on Sunday." She waited.

Presently the butler's voice came over the 'phone. Octavia smiled. "I may. Thank her Ladyship and tell her to expect us about one." She replaced the receiver, then put her arms round herself and gave herself a hug.

"There's a clever girl," she said out loud. "I think, dear David, when you see the little angel in her home setting you won't be quite so keen."

Sunday was a perfect day. Octavia sang as she turned her car out of the St. Cloud's gate. David looked at her in surprise.

"Whatever did you drag me there for. I had to listen to every word of what St. Cloud thinks about the government. The poor old boy's so deaf now he can't hear if you do argue."

Octavia looked smug.

"I know, but I think one ought to see them sometimes. They do enjoy it so."

David shook his head in bewilderment.

"Are you ill, my poor sweet? The few words I had with Milly St. Cloud were spent in her trying to find out what you wanted, for she knew you must want something or you wouldn't be there."

Octavia put her foot on the accelerator.

"Well, she was wrong."

They drove through Horley and Redhill, to the outskirts of Coulsden. There the car slowed down.

"What's up?" asked David.

"Look!" Octavia pointed to the radiator from which steam was escaping. There was an ominous knocking.

"Boiling."

She nodded.

"That fool of a chauffeur must have forgotten to fill it." She turned suddenly to the right. "I know a garage."

"Where?"

She looked at him out of the corner of her eye to see how he took the answer.

"Mercia Lane, I think it's called." With relief she saw there was no sign of interest. So Annabel had kept her background to herself. Just what she had expected. "This is it I think." She took a right hand turn. Slowly they cruised up the road. But no garage. "What an idiot I am. I must have got the wrong street." She eyed the numbers and drew up at 110. "Better ask these people to give us water, or we shall blow up."

Unwillingly David got out.

"I hate disturbing people on Sunday afternoons. But I suppose I must." He opened the gate, went up to the front door, and rang.

Chapter Six

ETHEL liked Sunday afternoons. She liked the spring and summer ones best. Afternoons like this one, with George messing about outside, calling to her through the window:

"My word, Ethel, these lilies will be a show. Don't know where they've all come from, I'm sure there's more than we put in."

Alfie and Maudie helping their father. Alfie very grand on the garden steps tying back the rambler. Maudie clipping the grass edge with an old pair of scissors. So happy to be allowed to help that she kept up a tuneless moan which was her way of singing. Lorna sitting on the window ledge, her jersey undone at the neck and pulled down as far as it would go. Ethel smiled tolerantly. Lorna was a funny one and no mistake, but if she wanted to sunbathe like those people in the picture papers why shouldn't she? Through the half open kitchen door she could see Annabel. She was curled up in the big armchair stitching at one of those flimsy things that passed for underclothes at Bertna's. She was wearing an old pull-over and skirt. To Ethel's mind she looked much nicer dressed that way, much more like the child she had nursed through measles and whooping-cough. Dressed as she was all the week she looked so got up she didn't like her to come out in the kitchen for a gossip as she had done in her less grand days. Those gossips while the supper was cooking had been nice, she missed them.

Ethel sang as she walked about her kitchen. An odd collection of tunes, varying from "Abide with me" to "The big bad wolf." Ever since she had married she had managed something special for Sunday tea. Even in the bad years when they made the cut at Fordwych's, and that even worse time when Alfie was ill, costing more than they could manage, she had never failed on Sunday tea. There was always a big home-made cake, and most weeks a plate of hot scones, but as well there was a "special." This week she had got something they would all like. A nice big dish of shrimps, as fresh as if you'd caught them yourself. Made you think of summer even to sniff them. There was one of those sticky brown loaves and plenty of butter to go with them. Even Alfie would eat properly when he'd got a slice of bread and butter piled high with shrimps.

The kettle boiled. Ethel poured a drop of water into the pot to warm it, then she leant out of the window:

"Come on, you gardeners. Just time to wash before tea. I've put all your shoes on the mat. Don't let me catch any of you bringing that earth into the house."

She opened her caddy and spooned the tea into the pot, with one ear towards the other room to hear her family's pleasure over the shrimps. She did not have long to wait. Maudie's shrill:

"Swimps for tea. Swimps. Look, Alfie, there's swimps."

Alfie's:

"Gosh, I'm hungry." (Ethel gave a grateful smile to heaven for that.)

George's measured:

"Feeling a bit peckish myself. Nothing like gardening to give you an appetite."

Lorna's rather la-di-da voice. How Ethel wished she wouldn't think that mincing tone was smart. All the children spoke nicely by nature, funny she couldn't hear how terrible that surburban-refined was.

"I like shrimps, but they do make a mess of your fingers."

Ethel would have enjoyed popping her head round the door with a nice snappy phrase, but she had no time, they were all at Lorna:

"No one wants you to eat them."

"If Lorna doesn't want them, there's more swimps for us."

George's scornful:

"Afraid of messing your fingers with them, same as you are of a bit of clean earth." He turned to Annabel. "You're not worrying about your hands, are you, my girl?"

Ethel had just picked up the teapot. She paused, straining for the answer. George meant that as an olive branch. He was trying hard, feeling his way so as to have things between him and Annabel back where they were before. Poor George! As if they ever could be. Only a man would be blind enough not to see.

"Course not, Dad." Annabel's voice had the "couple of kids together" note it used to have when she and her father caught the same train and won a tin of toffee. "Bet you I eat more of them than you do."

Ethel brought in the teapot. George stood up. He knew it was old-fashioned, but at any meal when they were all together he liked to say grace:

"For what we are about to receive may the Lord make us truly thankful."

"Well, if He always sends shrimps we shall be." Lorna helped herself to a handful.

George flushed. He disliked this modern way of making light of holy things. Besides, there was no excuse for his children. He had taken them to church himself since they were tinies. Ethel saw he was upset.

"That's no way to speak, Lorna, and you know it." She turned to George. "It's great, the lilies are coming on like that."

George was side-tracked just as she had hoped.

"You'll find it a bit of all right, old lady, sitting out for tea with the smell of your own lilies all round you."

Alfie giggled.

"Better than last time we had tea out."

They laughed. Last time they had tea outside was in September, the day they had come back from their holidays. At Bognor they had got used to being out all day. That first afternoon at home they had felt shut in, and tea outside seemed a reminder of tea on the beach with sand on the cake, and the scent of seaweed in their noses. But no sooner had they sat down than they sniffed. Ethel had made a face.

"Whatever is it?"

"Something's dead," Annabel had suggested.

George (who was still in a bit of a holiday mood) had turned to Alfie:

"What about seeing this scouting we've heard so much about. You go and scout that smell."

How they had all laughed. Even now the memory of it set them off. Alfie on his hands and knees snuffing round the garden with his nose to the ground. Then his sudden cry of triumph and the finding of the kipper. No one had ever known how it got there.

"Don't you remind me of that, Alfie." Ethel wiped her eyes. "I can see you now, holding it by the tail. I never knew a kipper could turn like that."

Annabel spoke through her laughter.

"Do you remember Maudie thought it had followed us from Bognor?"

Alfie choked.

"And Lorna told us how it had taken a railway ticket and then a taxi."

They roared at the memory of that silly afternoon. Suddenly through the noise they heard the bell.

"S-sh!" Ethel held up her hand. "There's someone at the door."

"It's the kipper," Alfie suggested.

They all giggled. Ethel nodded at Lorna.

"Go and see who it is, dear." She turned to George. "Funny on a Sunday afternoon."

Lorna left the door open. They sat in silence, listening. Lorna opened the front door. A man's voice said:

"I'm so sorry to bother you—" No one was looking at Annabel or they would have seen her start and gasp. A drawling woman's voice broke in:

"This is Lord de Bett. He wants—"

"Are you David de Bett?" Lorna asked. "I didn't know you were a lord. Annabel never told us that."

At the table they were all staring at Annabel. Ethel pulled herself together and smiled at her.

"Go along, dear. Bring your friends in. Alfie, get two chairs. I'll fetch the cups and plates."

Annabel was stunned into silence. What was David doing here? Why had he brought Octavia?

Ethel saw she was going to be no help. She touched George on the shoulder. "You get the things. I'll go to the door."

Ethel was slightly disturbed by learning of David's title, but no sign of that showed in her face as she moved Lorna aside and came to the front door. She held out her hand:

"How do you do. I'm Annabel's mother. I'm glad you've been able to come along at last. I've told her to bring you in I don't know how many times."

David shook her hand.

"How do you do, Mrs. Brown? This is Miss Glaye. Annabel has often asked me to come to tea, but I've never managed it. But to-day I was in this part." He caught the sound of Octavia drawing in her breath. He gave her a sharp kick on the ankle to keep her quiet. "I was in Miss Glaye's car, so I brought her along, too. I hope it's all right."

Ethel beamed at him. She was sorry he was a peer. She had rather Annabel took up with some boy living round about. But she saw at once that David was a man she could get on with.

"Come in. I hope you like shrimps."

"Shrimps!" David's face lit up. Not since he had grown up had anyone offered him shrimps for tea. "You couldn't offer me anything I like better."

Ethel opened the door of the sitting-room. She gripped Lorna with one hand to prevent her pushing in first. David hung back to let Octavia pass him. As she passed, he whispered:

"Behave, or I'll murder you . . ."

David sat between Annabel and Ethel. As he took his seat he gave Annabel's hand a reassuring squeeze, but he could feel she was too confused to realise what it meant. He did not wonder she was puzzled. All this talk about asking him to tea, when the poor child had never even told him where she lived. Breathing venom on Octavia, he hurled himself into conversation with Ethel.

"Shrimps have the best memories for me. I was one of those children who always got a bad report at school. I used to come cringing home for the holidays, knowing that presently I would face my mother, who would say, 'David, what is the meaning of this?' But I never had to have that interview without first being fortified. We had a housekeeper called Mrs. Edwards, and she always had tea with shrimps waiting for me in the housekeeper's room." He looked across at Alfie. "Do you wonder I like shrimps?"

"Gosh! No." Alfie looked at him sympathetically.

Lorna, who knew herself to be the black sheep of the family, was delighted to find the only peer she knew in the same position.

"Did your mother punish you for your bad reports?"

"Yes. Regularly as clockwork I was told that something especially nice had been planned for the next day, and now it wouldn't happen."

"What a shame." Ethel handed the shrimps to him. He already had plenty on his plate, but she felt she must make up to him in some way for those holiday treats he had never had.

"I shouldn't pity him." Octavia's voice was so venomous that all the Browns except Annabel looked at her in surprise. "He's had what he wanted ever since"—she gave Annabel a glance of faked sympathy "—and sometimes I think he pays back old scores to make up for his childhood."

"Dear me," thought Ethel, "don't care for her. Pity, with that lovely face. Looks like the Virgin on that church calendar we had last Christmas. Got a fit of sulks like Lorna gets. Liver, like as not." If it was liver, she was sorry for Octavia, but she was not going to have her or anybody else spoiling Sunday tea. She gave her a friendly nod, as if she had said something nice, and turned to David.

"You fond of lilies? My husband's trying them this year."

George had been tongue-tied since the guests appeared. He had known that some day Annabel would have a young man. If he had been honest with himself he would have admitted that deep in his soul he dreaded his coming. He wanted his family to himself, with no outsiders interfering. But the worst he had pictured was some boy from round about, coming in and out, trying to get Annabel alone to give her a kiss. But this Lord de Bett, what was he here for? He was the same sort as Mr. Ian Fordwych. A very nice young man to have as the boss's son, but not the sort you wanted dropping in for Sunday tea. As for Octavia, he had never been so scared of anybody. There was something so cherished about her appearance that it made him feel his home was not good enough for her. This annoyed him, for he knew his home was good enough for anybody. Besides, to be cherished as Octavia looked as if she had been, he was sure was not good for anybody. He had hoped both guests would go quickly, so he need not say anything to them. Then Ethel must go dragging him into the conversation with her chat about lilies. As if a man like this Lord de Bett could be interested in his little bit of garden. He probably had a place half the size of Kensington Gardens.

"I've only a few," he explained apologetically.

David was interested.

"Lilies? Now, what sort are you trying? I grew masses last year, but they weren't a success. Either I flew too high or it was a bad year."

George lit up with a gardener's eagerness. He forgot that David had probably thousands of lilies and he only twelve (though more than that seemed to be coming up), he was merely face-to-face with a man who was failing with a crop with which he looked like doing well.

"What's your soil?"

This was too much. Octavia had not brought David here to talk about lilies with Annabel's father. She leant forward.

"What a *poseur* you are, David. Trying to pretend you know what goes on in your garden. You know really you leave it entirely to your gardeners." She turned laughingly to Annabel. "He is deceitful, isn't he? To hear him, you would have thought he'd dropped into tea this afternoon at your invitation, while really he had no idea where you lived, and certainly had never thought of coming here."

Ethel tried desperately to save the situation.

"What nonsense, Miss Glaye. Then why did he come?"

"Because, coming back from lunch, we ran out of water for the car, and he said: 'Let's ask one of these comic little houses to give us some.'"

Octavia's words cut through the lethargy into which this totally incomprehensible visit had thrown Annabel. "Comic little house!" What a way to speak of her home before Mum and Dad. She got up.

"Right. I'll get you the water, and then you can go. This house may seem funny to you, but we're happy in it"—she looked at Ethel—"aren't we, Mum? You may have thought it was clever bringing David here, but it wasn't. I wanted him to come, but I didn't like to ask him and—" She broke off, for to her horror she began to cry.

David patted her shoulder.

"It's all right, sweet; no need for heroics. You can trust your Uncle David to deal with this." He shook Ethel's hand. "We shall be meeting again. I've enjoyed coming here enormously but I expect we'd better go."

Octavia, with a general smile such as her mother used when opening a bazaar, turned to the door.

"Good-bye. Thank you so much for the tea."

"Alfie," said George, "take out a big jug of water and fill up their radiator."

David looked back into the sitting-room. He saw Ethel had her arms round Annabel. A tender expression that had not been there before was in his eyes. He said apologetically to George:

"I can't expect you to believe it, but I didn't know Annabel lived here. But perhaps now I do, you'll have the generosity to forgive this afternoon and let me come again. Good-bye."

Annabel heard the car start. She pulled free from Ethel and watched it disappear down the road. Then, without a word, she turned and ran up to her bedroom and locked the door.

Ethel began to clear the tea. Suddenly she laughed.

"That was a funny Sunday tea."

George shook his head anxiously at the ceiling.

"She's upset."

Ethel giggled.

"I know. But it did me good to hear her tell that Miss Glaye where she got off." She beckoned to her family. "You know I'm not a one for punishments, but the first of you that mentions him or her to Annabel will get something they don't like."

Until they were round the corner Octavia and David sat in silence. Then David said:

"Drop me at the first bus, tube or tram you see."

"Why?" Octavia put her foot on the accelerator. "You're not in a fuss are you? It was only a joke."

"Joke!" He looked at her with a cruelly clear eye. "You've enough looks to wreck a thousand ships, Octavia. But I saw this afternoon a thing I've long suspected. You've no heart. And I learnt too you've never heard the word 'good manners.' There's a bus. Good-bye."

Octavia stopped the car.

"Surely you're not going to quarrel with me over a little shop girl?"

He sighed.

"Quarrel? No. I'm saying good-bye."

He got out and crossed the street.

Chapter Seven

ELIZABETH was lying on her chair. Freda sat on the end of it. There were crimson patches on her cheeks.

"It's the injustice that gets me. Because I slip down the stairs in one of the models to talk to a friend there's no need to speak to me the way Miss Petoff did."

"It's a shame," Elizabeth agreed.

"I suppose us girls must be allowed to speak to our friends sometimes. I wonder she doesn't shut us up in convents right away and have done with it."

Elizabeth giggled.

"You'd be a scream in a convent."

Freda was too angry to see the funny side of anything.

"Tony was only here a minute, just long enough to arrange about to-night."

"Did Miss Petoff catch you talking?"

Freda wriggled.

"Not so much talking. I suppose it's up to us girls whether we kiss our friends or not. Or does Bertna's think they've bought us?"

Obviously if you were found kissing on the stairs there must be trouble. Elizabeth could think of nothing better to say than to repeat:

"It's a shame."

"I wouldn't mind so much," Freda raged, "if it wasn't for the injustice. She said 'I'm always having trouble of this sort with you and Elizabeth.'"

Elizabeth sighed at the truth of this statement.

"They shouldn't be so nosey."

"Nosey!" Freda sniffed. "They're not nosey enough. I nearly said that to Miss Petoff. I nearly said 'Suppose you stop spying on Elizabeth and me for a bit and have a look at Bernadette and Annabel. You'll be surprised at what you'll find.'"

Elizabeth sat up.

"What would she? Have you found where Bernadette goes in that Rolls?"

Freda got up and went to the cupboard. She mixed herself a bromo seltzer.

"Not yet, but I will. But I could tell you something about Annabel which would surprise you."

"I bet you don't. You said the other day you were keeping it to yourself."

Freda stirred her bromo seltzer thoughtfully. She had made five pounds out of what she knew. It was unlikely there was any more in it.

"She goes out with Lord de Bett."

"What!" Elizabeth was so surprised that for a moment she could not collect her wits. "Are you sure?"

Freda nodded.

"I'd love to see our dear Octavia's face if she knew."

"She does know." Freda's voice took on a note of righteous indignation. "It's a shame. To think that one of us from this room should behave like that. And then Miss Petoff dares to say it's always you and me."

The gross unfairness suddenly struck Elizabeth:

"My word! It is a nerve. And us two the only decent ones most likely."

"If Miss Petoff knew," Freda broke in, stimulated to flights of fancy by her bromo seltzer, "she'd have to apologise to us on her knees."

Elizabeth nodded:

"And give both the others the sack."

Bernadette came in. She raised her eyebrows to Freda in sympathetic enquiry.

"Did she give you hell?"

Freda gave her a dirty look.

"Yes. But if she knew what I knew it wouldn't be me that was getting it."

Bernadette's head was inside the dress she had been showing. She pulled it off and began to put on another:

"Wonderful imagination you've got. I expect it's all that fizzy drink. Something ought to be inflated by now goodness knows."

Freda looked sourly at the door through which Bernadette had departed but she said nothing. Then suddenly there was a gleam in her eyes. By keeping her eyes open she had made five pounds out of Annabel. By keeping those same eyes glued what might there not be made out of Bernadette. She whistled softly.

Elizabeth lay and stared at the ceiling. So that was the reason for the change in Annabel. Going out with David de Bett. No wonder she could afford new clothes. Probably gave her money. She would make it her business to find out.

Annabel came hurrying in.

"You're to show the rust chiffon, Freda."

Freda took off her dressing gown.

"You've been a time. Who is it?"

"Somebody's grand-daughter who's getting married." She stepped out of the black net she was wearing and hung it on a hanger.

Freda turned her back to her:

"Do me up. You showing anything else?"

"Not if she likes that. I expect she will. She wants that colour."

Annabel fastened Freda's hooks, then thankfully lay in her chair and shut her eyes.

Three days since Sunday. She knew he had gone to the country. He had told her last week he would be going. But with that awful tea hanging over her memory she would have been so glad of even a word with him. Not that she was afraid. He must have guessed the kind of home that she came from. That they were quite simple people. After all, they were only friends. She might be silly enough to love him, but of course he did not know that. Naturally any thought of his loving her was ridiculous. Besides there was Octavia. It was the thought that she had looked ridiculous on Sunday afternoon that was frightening her. Their friendship was such a slender thing. It would be so easy for him never to see her again. In London he found her a change.

He thought it funny that anybody could be like her, never drinking nor smoking, and not understanding the point of stories Daphne told. But she had a suspicion that on Sunday she had stopped seeming amusing and was just a gawk. Standing up there answering Miss Glaye back wasn't the sort of thing his sort of people did. She had tried so hard too to be more like his sort of people. She had found out all about Magdalen, and the right way to talk of people who had titles, and lots of other things, like what M.F.H. meant, which she had never known before. But what was the good. That awful Sunday tea had probably spoilt everything.

"So our little Annabel has made friends with Lord de Bett," said Elizabeth softly.

Annabel felt as though she had been suddenly ducked in icy water.

"I haven't. How did you know? I mean we aren't friends. We're only—"

"Only what?"

Annabel tried to think of a word which would cover the dog-like devotion on her side, and the laughing elder brother attitude on his.

"We just know each other."

Elizabeth sniffed.

"Well I suppose everything's got to begin somewhere, and if you don't care where it ends."

Annabel, miserably conscious that it might have ended last Sunday, looked puzzled for Elizabeth could not know about that.

"I don't see why friends can't go on being friends." Even to herself this sounded rather a lame statement.

Elizabeth studied her.

"Can you really be as simple as you pose to be? I should open my eyes if I were you, my dear. When the evening comes that you are asked to go back to the flat 'just for a drink' don't forget the gipsy's warning."

Bernadette came in.

"You're to show the green net, Elizabeth." She looked quickly at Annabel's face. What had Elizabeth been talking about? There was certainly an atmosphere in the room. The moment the door closed she came across to her.

"What was Elizabeth saying?"

Annabel looked at her wretchedly:

"She sort of said that men who get to know girls like us were expecting—" she broke off. "But it isn't true."

Since last week, when she had seen Annabel with David, Bernadette had been waiting for just this opening.

"Models rank with the chorus in lots of men's minds, and they are considered gay. It's a hang over from the naughty nineties, when chorus girls led the life. I think they still hope we aren't fussy to put it mildly."

Annabel's mouth was scornful:

"You can't really think that. Not nice men. It's idiotic. I suppose one can be friends with people."

Bernadette felt she was making a mess of things. In Annabel's state it was easy to get angry at one hint of criticism of the beloved. She stooped and patted her hand.

"All right. But if you would listen to your old aunt Bernadette, you'd watch your step. Of course there is no harm in going out to meals and to dance. Only if ever a suggestion came of tea in the flat, or such, I'd be careful."

At 110 Mercia Lane there was a lot of brooding over Sunday.

"He seemed a nice enough young fellow," George said to Ethel, "But he's not our sort. What's he after?"

Ethel was brushing her hair at the time. She stopped and swung round on her chair:

"Nothing. His coming was none of his doing."

"I know that Miss Glaye got him here." George sat down on the bed with a worried frown. He took off his shoes. "But why?"

Ethel gave a sniff. It was a nice long satisfying sound and expressed a lot of what she thought of Octavia.

"The way I read it is this. She—" she gave a contemptuous jerk of her thumb to indicate Octavia. "wants to marry him. Our Annabel has got in her way."

"Well, if she has, why bring him here?"

Ethel gave him a tolerant smile. Funny she often thought what great babies men were.

"Well, old dear, this isn't exactly Sandringham. Wanted him to see where Annabel belongs."

George bristled.

"There's nothing we need be ashamed of."

Ethel went on with her brushing. There was a faint smile round her lips.

"Nothing. My word he enjoyed his shrimps." George padded across to her in his socks.

"That may be. But what's he want with Annabel?" Ethel's face grew serious. She looked in the mirror. Her reflection was there and so was George's. But she saw neither of them. Instead she saw a little scene she had often pictured. Sunday morning and her cooking the dinner. Then one of them calling from the other room: 'Here they come, Mum.' She running out to the front of the house, and watching Annabel, and the man who would be Annabel's husband, coming down the road pushing a perambulator in which was her grandson. The vision faded. She looked up at George's reflection. Such a worried face. Besides he had taken off his collar. There was something about George or Alfie without a collar that always got her. They looked so defenceless somehow. She gave him a reassuring smile:

"I don't know, old dear. All I know is we've brought her up all right. We can't do more."

"We can refuse to let her see him."

Ethel shook her head.

"We couldn't, and it wouldn't be sense if we could. Its my own belief there's nothing in this, not on his side anyway."

"Then he's no right to go upsetting Annabel."

Ethel laughed.

"You've forgotten human nature. You can't stop a girl falling in love. Any more than you can make a man see what's under his nose. I reckon he doesn't know."

"What'll happen to Annabel when she finds there's nothing in it?"

Ethel picked up the comb. Thoughtfully she ran her finger up and down the teeth.

"I think she's always known that. But knowing you were going to hurt yourself never yet stopped a woman from loving." She turned round and laid her hand on George's arm. "But there's one thing I do know. We mustn't interfere. When the time comes that she doesn't see him any more she'll have quite enough to put up with, without she has to feel her Mum and Dad had a share in breaking things."

Sunday's tea had shown Lorna a new world. She had been jealous of Annabel with her clothes, and going to smart hotels. But it was a childish sort of jealousy. She could neither imagine the insides of the hotels nor the sort of people Annabel might meet. Then suddenly two of them had appeared in the flesh. To Lorna it was not David who was exciting, though of course it was fun having a Lord to tea and something to tell the girls about. The thrill was Octavia. Never in her wildest dreams had she pictured anyone like her. From the soles of her feet to the top of her head she thought her perfect. Mentally she fell down and worshipped. Those few words that Octavia had said she thought divine. In just that proud cutting way the aristocracy ought to talk. She felt such adoration that she could not bring herself to discuss Octavia with her girl friends. In the whole of Lorna's school life this was the first thing she had felt unable to discuss. But admiration was not the only quality Lorna felt. She had not been to the pictures for nothing. She knew that girls could rise to the top no matter where they started. "That's me" she told herself. "When I'm grown-up somehow I'll be like her."

It was on the Wednesday following the Sunday tea that Lorna got her invitation. There was a family called Williams living not far from them who had rather more money than their neighbours. Neither George nor Ethel cared much for the family, they thought their style of dressing loud, and their whole manner of living ostentatious. In this they were backed by Annabel who, after one visit to the house, had refused to go again.

"I don't like them, Mum. They're always telling you how much everything cost."

Alfie had stubbornly set his face against going near them.

"What? Go to tea with that cissy-looking Leonard? Not me."

But Lorna adored being asked. She thought it was just like her family's stupid stuffiness not to appreciate the only smart people they knew. This invitation was to a real party. Poppy Williams, who was just her age, was having a birthday.

"Mum." Lorna was pink with pleasure. "There's a party at the Williams's on Saturday week."

Ethel was busy laying the supper. She knew just how Lorna regarded the Williams, so she wasted no time in argument.

"That's nice, dear."

"Mum." Lorna caught her by the arm. "I must have a new dress for it, there'll be dancing."

Ethel never spoke to the children without thinking first, but she knew the answer to this one. New clothes came to them all quite fairly. When things were going well, Lorna had new school clothes of some sort each winter and a new summer frock or two in time for the holiday, and there was always a dress for parties. At present the party dress was green velvet, it had been Annabel's, but it was still good.

"You can't, dear. Not this time of year. Perhaps next winter. I'll steam it up for you."

"Steam it up!" It seemed to Lorna that she must be the only girl in the world with a mother quite so devoid of clothes sense.

"But it's awful. And it's too tight. Anyway, I wore it there before, and Poppy's certain to have a new frock."

Ethel smiled at her sympathetically.

"I wish I could manage it. But you've grown so I'm having to get you all new things for the summer. I'm afraid the green'll have to do just once more." She heard her kettle boiling and went into the kitchen.

Lorna opened her mouth to speak. Then, with her eyes full of tears, she ran upstairs. She sat down on her bed and glared miserably at the wall.

She wouldn't wear it. She wouldn't. Other girls had nice things, why shouldn't she? Look at Annabel. Three new frocks since Christmas and all these underclothes. She'd rather not go than wear that awful old dress. If only she could have something new she'd show those Williams a thing or two. She'd have something like Octavia would have worn at her age.

Annabel came in. She had walked up from the station with a dispirited droop to her shoulders.

The afternoon conversations were nagging at her in spite of herself. She would not have minded Elizabeth. But Bernadette! It was not true, of course. Bernadette didn't know David. But she did wish she hadn't said what she had said. Her friendship with David was so light a thing, these hints were like smuts on a flower. Just outside the front door she pulled herself together. Mustn't let Mum see her with a long face.

"Hullo, dear." Ethel came out into the hall and kissed her. "You look tired. Run up and wash and come and sit by the fire. Dad's out in the garden. I'll have supper ready in five minutes." Annabel turned to go, but Ethel caught her by the arm. She spoke in a whisper. "Try and put Lorna in a good temper; she's upset."

"What about?"

"She wants a new dress to wear at a party at the Williams's."

"What, them!" Annabel made a face. "I wouldn't put on clean stockings to go there."

"I know." Ethel grinned at her in complete agreement. "But she doesn't feel like that. Besides"—she squeezed Annabel's arm—"all the nice things you have now make it a bit difficult for Lorna."

Annabel was surprised. She had not thought of this.

"I never had them when I was her age."

"I know." Ethel turned to go back to the kitchen. "But nor did anyone else in the house. There's a lot in that." She paused, smiling. "Why, it's even getting me. I wasted half the afternoon trying to re-trim my best hat. That's all your doing, coining home dressed up like the Duchess of Kent." She jerked her thumb up the stairs. "Say what you can, it does upset Dad so when she sulks at the table."

Annabel stood in the bedroom door and smiled at her sister.

"Hullo. What are you doing up here?"

Lorna raked Annabel's figure. She had on the new green. She knew David was in the country, but there was always the chance he might come back.

"The Williams's are having a dance," Lorna burst out. "It's Saturday week, and Mum won't give me a new frock. She says I've got to wear that awful old green."

Annabel looked sympathetic.

"I'm sorry. I expect she can't manage it just now. I wish I could help, but I got my salary advanced to get my new things. Besides, it's a silly time of year for that sort of thing. It's between seasons."

Lorna scowled.

"I bet the girls who dress at Bertna's have new dresses for parties all the year."

Annabel laughed.

"People of your age don't dress there. Except when they're bridesmaids or something like that."

Weddings always interested Lorna.

"Do they have lovely things as bridesmaids?" Annabel came and sat on the bed beside her.

"At a wedding this week they're four girls just about your age. They're having silk organdie over taffeta. It's got blue flowers on it, and they have wide blue sashes to match. They do look sweet."

Lorna heaved a deep sigh. Organdie and taffeta! What wouldn't she give to be dressed like that.

Annabel opened her bag.

"Look, here's half a crown. It's not much, but I'm short. But you can get some stockings. They have good seconds for that."

Lorna looked at the half-crown. It wouldn't go far towards organdie, but it was something. She gave Annabel a hug and, outwardly comforted, went down to supper.

Chapter Eight

IT WAS Saturday afternoon. David was still in the country. The sun never seemed to shine properly when he was away, but Annabel, as she left Bertna's, could see it was a lovely day. Bernadette came down the steps beside her.

"What are you doing this afternoon?"

"Nothing particular."

Bernadette pointed at the sky.

"Good thing in the way of days. Besides, as Freda would say, 'us girls don't get much air.' Would you like to come with me to Kew?"

There was really nothing except to see David that Annabel did want to do, but, failing that, it would be nice to be with Bernadette.

The girls ate at Lyons' Corner House, then took a bus. Annabel had not been to Kew before. It was at that moment when the Japanese cherries lie like pink clouds against the skyline, and silent people walk round them convinced it must be a dream and not their fate to see such beauty. Bernadette and Annabel stared with the rest. At last Bernadette moved away.

"Let's go and sit under a tree and have a nice plebeian cigarette. One more look at that tree and I shall grow sentimental, and I'm repulsive in that state."

They found an oak with curling roots just shaped to sit on. Bernadette looked up at the branches overhead. Suddenly she giggled.

"I wonder if Freda has come with us."

Annabel, whose mind was on David, looked up startled.

"Why should she have?"

Bernadette lit a cigarette.

"She's been following me."

"What for?"

"Oh, I don't know." Bernadette buried her match in the grass. "She's got a naturally copper's-nark streak." There was a silence. Freda and her silliness seemed a long way away. They dropped her out of the conversation as obviously misplaced. Annabel stared at the young green of the trees. Where was David at this moment? His place in the country must be something like this, only, of course, not open to the public. Funny, if just at this moment he was sitting under a tree, only, of course, he wouldn't be thinking of her.

Bernadette lay back and listened to a lark. When at last she spoke her head was still raised to the sky.

"I've been wanting a word with you ever since Wednesday." Annabel stiffened. Bernadette sensed this, but she went on unmoved. "It's difficult when you want to say something not to say too much. I'm afraid I laboured my point a bit the other day."

Annabel played with her fingers and flushed.

"No, you didn't, but you've got it all wrong. I know you all think there's always marriage or—"

She paused embarrassed for words. Bernadette gave a gesture with her hand.

"It's all right, I'm following you. No need to explain."

"But this time it isn't like that. David and I are just friends. Of course, he wouldn't marry me, but he isn't a bit like Elizabeth and Freda expect men to be. He's more like a brother."

Bernadette went on smoking and staring skywards.

"Freda and Elizabeth have minds like a couple of drains. All the same, life being what it is, it's difficult to retain the brother-and-sister angle. At least, that's been my experience."

"I'll have to manage to," Annabel explained simply, "because I expect he's marrying Octavia, and anyway, of course, it won't be me."

Bernadette flicked some ash off her cigarette.

"You're in love with him."

It was a statement, not a question. It did not even embarrass Annabel. To hear the words, "In love with him," spoken made her happy. Without prevarication she said:

"Yes."

There was another long silence. This time it was full of friendliness. Then Bernadette seemed to come to a decision. She sat up and hugged her knees.

"I came to Bertna's two years ago. I came straight from a convent. Between you and me, I had something of a history, which only Miss Petoff knew. One day at a party I met somebody like your David. His name's Jim. I did just what you've done. I fell up to the chin in love. He treated me as though I was his sister, and so I thought the friendship would go on like that. In my case the shock came from something much more surprising than what we suggest may happen to you. He asked me to marry him. You've no idea what a shock it was. He's not like David, heir to a property and last of a long line of dreary peers, but he is fabulously rich. He makes cars. Model works. Honour and fairness his gods. You know the type. If I'd thought, I suppose I might have guessed he was the marrying sort. But, somehow, hearing the girls talking at Bertna's, I'd forgotten that his type existed. You'll think that odd after my warning you about David. But he's differently placed. With his history there's a lot more to it. He has to marry his own kind."

Annabel rolled over on to her elbows.

"If you love him, why haven't you married him?"

Bernadette made an expressive face.

"That, my sweet, is exactly what I have brought you to Kew to hear. You see, I was drifting along with a platonic friendship. I was happy, and wouldn't think what the next step might be going to be. Then one night he asked me to marry him. It was the loveliest moment I'll ever know. I said 'Yes,' and then I cried. I suppose seeing me crying made him think what a kid I was. He asked me if I'd any family he could fix up with."

"Had you?"

Savagely Bernadette stubbed out her cigarette on the grass and buried it under a handful of earth.

"I can't tell you that side of the story. There are reasons. Lord isn't my real name, and I thought if he knew who I was it would finish everything. If only I'd looked ahead, I'd have realised that friendships between men and women aren't possible, and some sort of proposal was coming. But I hadn't, so I lost my head, lied, and said my father was abroad."

"And he wasn't?"

"No. Of course, Jim, who's a business man, started at once. 'Where is he?' 'Let's cable.' Anyway, it didn't take him long to see I was lying. He went away."

Annabel looked puzzled.

"Then who does the Rolls belong to?" Bernadette laughed.

"Shop gossip's a bit inaccurate. It isn't a Rolls. But it's Jim's. We met again last year. He was awfully nice. He said couldn't we see each other, but he didn't feel it was any good beginning being married with secrets between us, and when I felt like telling him about myself, he was ready."

Annabel felt it was not her place to make suggestions. All the same, the story sounded a bit as if Bernadette was being silly.

"But if he loves you, would he mind whatever it is you haven't told him?"

Bernadette nodded.

"Last Christmas I meant to tell him. Then we met a man he knew. Something was said which made me know there were things he'd never forgive. Besides, if I was going to tell him the beginning was the time. Sometimes I think now that if I'd only not been taken by surprise I would have. That's where my bedtime story touches you. This brother-and-sister stuff will stop one day. I know you've nothing to hide, but you may be faced with a decision. Well, do give yourself time. Make up your mind what you are going to do before it happens."

Annabel raised her eyes to Bernadette's.

"Do you mean you think David will want me to be more than friends?"

Bernadette nodded.

Annabel laughed.

"Of course I couldn't. But he won't ask me. He's not a bit like that."

Bernadette got up.

"It's getting cold. Come on. I'll accept that David won't, but, to please me, think about what you will do if he does. You see, you'll need all your courage. Saying 'No' would probably mean saying 'Good-bye.' Shall we have some tea?"

Annabel looked at her shyly.

"I suppose you wouldn't come back and have it with us, would you?"

"Would I! Come on." Bernadette took her arm. "Is your mother the kind who would let us have dripping toast?"

In the train Annabel told Bernadette about last Sunday's tea. To her surprise, Bernadette found it very funny. She rocked with laughter, and kept making Annabel repeat bits.

"'What a *poseur* David is. To hear him, you would think he'd dropped in to tea this afternoon at your invitation.' Did Octavia really say that? I've always known she was the queen of the cats, but that wins. 'Water for the car.'" She went off into another paroxysm of laughter. "Goodness, I do wish I'd been there."

George, Ethel, Alfie and Maudie were having tea when the girls arrived. The house was trained to receiving girl friends by Lorna. George gave one quick look at Bernadette and decided if on the smart side she seemed a nice sensible sort. Ethel noticed the girl's pleased look when she saw it was a family party. 'Lonely' she thought. She got up.

"I'll put on a couple of eggs. You two could do with them after your walk."

Annabel caught hold of her dress:

"Do you know what Bernadette said when I asked her to tea? She said 'Is your mother the sort who would let us have dripping toast?'"

Ethel laughed happily.

"And me with a great bowl of dripping only wanting eating. You wait."

Of course with dripping toast on the table they all started tea over again. Even George had a bit although as he said it wasn't the thing for a man who was going to spend the evening gardening.

Bernadette told Maudie the story of the patient whose only cure was sea-foam on toast, and how difficult it was to keep foam on toast. She told Alfie that she had been brought up in the country, and next time she saw him she'd bring some elastic and show him how to make a special sort of catapult. She talked gardening to George, and though, as he said afterwards, it was easy to see she had known better days and been used to far more space than he bad, yet she had ideas and was fond of lilies. She threw little remarks to Ethel to show how well Annabel was doing at Bertna's, and hinted that she was being looked after. It was altogether a most successful tea. Then came the knock on the door. They stopped talking.

"There's that kipper again," said Alfie, but he was not a bit surprised when the joke fell flat. They looked at Annabel. She got up:

"You needn't all look at me like that. It's not for me this time. I expect it's a friend of Dad's. I'll go and see."

Ethel pushed her back into her seat.

"Don't you. You finish your tea. I shouldn't wonder if it's someone from the church about the jumble."

They listened while the door was opened. They heard a voice ask "Name of Brown?" Then they stopped listening. The voice was plainly not the voice of David. Nor was there any female voice breaking into sound like Octavia's. Alfie told Bernadette the full story of the kipper. He made it very funny, and they were all laughing when the door opened and Ethel came back. She shut the door and leant against it. Her face was grey.

George got up and led her to a chair.

"What is it, old girl? Who was it?"

Ethel tried to speak, but no sound came for a moment. Then she whispered:

"It was a policeman. It's Lorna. She's been caught shop-lifting."

Chapter Nine

"There's nothing so bad that you can't stand up to it," Ethel had often said. But when she had said it she had pictured poverty, illness, even death, but not disgrace. Not that one of her children should be a thief. Lorna was silly, they all knew that. But a thief!

It was Annabel who broke the stunned silence which had fallen on them. She knelt down by Ethel's chair and put her arms round her:

"Don't take it too hard, Mum."

George moved impatiently.

"There's some things you can't take too hard." Annabel looked at Bernadette. She felt that she was the only one to understand what she meant.

"I don't believe Lorna meant to steal. I mean I think she may have taken something, but it'll all be part of her silliness. I think it's me having clothes."

Bernadette nodded:

"I don't know Lorna, but there are children like that, Mrs. Brown. They want things so badly that they lose any sense of responsibility."

George was fumbling in his cash boxes for money.

"I don't see how that helps. Doesn't matter why she's done it. Where is she, Ethel? I'll go and fetch her and pay what's owing."

Ethel raised her head. She was still very pale, but her courage was coming back. She got up.

"She's in the manager's room at the shop. But I'm going, George." She gave him a look which was an attempt at a smile. "You might say something you'd be sorry for, you know what you are when you're upset."

Annabel patted George's arm.

"Mum's right. This is a woman's job. You let us go."

George moved to the door.

"Not this time it isn't. If it's a case of squaring the manager I'm the one."

"There isn't any squaring to be done." Ethel's voice wobbled. "They've got the dress back, but it seems they've had trouble shop-lifting lately. They've charged her. She'll have to come up at the juvenile court." She lowered her voice, "The constable's waiting. He'll come with us."

"Gosh!" Alfie turned red. "Have you got to walk there with him. With all the people round knowing?"

Bernadette gave him a sympathetic grin:

"You won't believe it, but they'll be nice about it."

Ethel put her arm through George's.

"What do the neighbours matter. It's Lorna." She looked pleadingly at George, "Would you go with the constable and see what you've got to do? Let Annabel and me fetch Lorna."

Maudie began to cry:

"Will they put Lorna in pwison?"

Bernadette sat her on her knee.

"Of course not. Daddy might have to pay some money just as a promise he'll bring her to the court when she's wanted. She'll be back to supper. And you and I and Alfie will cook it while they're all out." Ethel looked at her gratefully:

"Will you stay with them? I should be grateful. But there's no need to trouble with supper. I'll see to that."

George opened the door.

"We shan't feel like food."

That got Ethel.

"Being hungry never helped anybody." She looked at Alfie, "The meat's in the larder. And you know where to find the vegetables. You show Miss Lord."

The shop was some distance away. Ethel and Annabel took a bus. They sat side by side in silence. Annabel tried to clarify her thoughts. She knew that at the back of her mind she felt that this trouble was her fault. What had she said when Lorna had told her about the green dress? Had she been sympathetic? She had meant to be but she had not been really. She had felt that Lorna was expecting luxuries that she had not had at her age. But the blame to herself went deeper than that. It was not her fault that she had been made a model at Bertna's. It was not her fault that she had seen David and had dressed to please him. But at home had it made for happiness? It seemed as if you could go on being happy with the same old things, meeting the same sort of people, as long as all did it. But when one of the family stepped away, wore different clothes, knew different people, then it affected everybody else. She had not really changed to Dad, it was Dad who was getting self-conscious about himself because she had changed. Nothing of course could change Mum, but even she was smartening up and perhaps a bit more aware of her old curtains. But this Lorna business went deeper than that. A few months ago Lorna would have grumbled at the old velvet, but she would have worn it. In a way this mess of Lorna's was her fault. She turned impetuously to Ethel:

"In a way it's my fault."

Ethel had no need of long reasoning, she caught at once at what Annabel meant.

"Not your fault. But in a way you've made it happen. Not but what Lorna was always weak. Still, if you are as vain as she's always been, seeing the lovely things you wear now was bound to turn her head." She fiddled with the fingers of her gloves.

"I've been thinking I shouldn't wonder if this didn't turn out all for the best. It was time Lorna had a jolt."

"But they may send her to one of the reform schools."

Ethel nodded.

"They may. But seeing the home she comes from and all, and it being the first trouble she's been in, it's more likely they'll put her on probation or whatever they call it. What I'm wondering is what I'd best say to her."

Annabel stared unseeingly at an advertisement. She was not naturally imaginative, but in that moment she managed to get a dim vision of how Lorna must be feeling.

"Don't let's say anything about it. She'll be feeling so bad she won't want us making it worse."

Lorna was feeling bad. It seemed that one moment she had been talking and laughing, and the next plunged into an abyss of terror, worse even than the nightmares she had when her temperature was high with measles. She had beguiled a friend called Olive to come and look at party frocks with her. At the back of her mind were a dozen fairy tales. A rich man stopped and said, "You are so pretty, do choose a frock, I'd love to give it to you." She saw the counter catch fire, and, at risk of her life, put it out. A grateful management rewarded her with anything she liked to choose. A sad faced woman stopped her and said, "You are so like my little girl who died, may I buy you the sort of frock she loved to wear?" But the afternoon was disappointing. None of these things happened. She and Olive walked round the department given up to school-girls' clothes, and nobody took the slightest interest in them. Then suddenly she saw it. The dress was on a coat-hanger on a line of party frocks. She gripped Olive:

"Ooh, look! That's like some dresses Bertna's are making for a wedding this week." She fingered it. "It wouldn't take much stuff. I wish I could take it home and show it to Mum, she might copy it."

Olive laughed:

"I dare you to."

There was no one apparently looking. Partly for fun, partly because she was obsessed by her need for a frock, and had been prepared for a miracle, Lorna seized it, rolled it into a ball, and put it under her coat. Olive gave her one startled, horrified glance and vanished. The rest was a confused jumble. There had been a ghastly walk through the shop when she could think of nothing but the bulge under her coat. Then there was a hand on her shoulder and a voice saying:—"Would you come in here a moment, please?" She had dropped the frock and tried to run. She had given her name and address. She had heard someone telephone the police station. Then she had fainted.

When she came round from fainting the shop manager was kind. He seemed sorry he had rung up the police. He seemed sorry for her when the policeman came. He said he wished it rested with him, and he wouldn't charge her, but it wasn't his shop. It was his idea that, as she was still so wobbly after fainting, she had better stay there until her father or mother came to fetch her. He had given her some tea. After that she had been left alone, and the waiting had been awful. What would they do to her? Would she go to prison? What would they say when they came to fetch her, particularly Dad? At last, after what seemed hours, she heard Ethel's voice outside. She shrank back against the horsehair sofa on which she was lying. The door opened and she saw her mother' face. Not angry of anything like that, just white and unhappy. Lorna gave a cry and flung herself into her arms.

Nobody likes Mondays. Annabel went into Bertna's feeling extra Mondayish. However hard they had tried to behave as usual at home, of course they had not been able to. Lorna had crept about not saying a word and looking like a ghost. George had insisted on them going to church, and though, as it happened, the news about Lorna had not yet got about, they all felt it had, and sat looking so hang-dog that everybody went home, and said: "What on earth's the matter with the Browns?" The rest of Sunday had seemed interminable. Lorna made things worse by having a crying fit in the evening which upset Maudie, who joined in. All of them were thankful when it was time for bed.

With the strain of Saturday and Sunday, Annabel felt anything but in the mood for work. Unfortunately she was not the only one to feel like that. Freda arrived looking ghastly.

"Oh, dear, what champagne can do to a girl if she takes one over the odds. I'm going to be sick."

Bernadette, who was herself white with shadows of sleeplessness under her eyes, looked up from her undressing:

"Not in here, I hope." She studied Freda with an experienced eye. "Better lie down and I'll mix you a bromo seltzer."

Freda gulped. She lay flat and shut her eyes.

"I couldn't face it."

Elizabeth came over and examined her. She raised inquiring eyes to Bernadette, who nodded:

"Better get it over, I should say. Someone's coming in for a lot of clothes this morning."

Elizabeth helped Freda to her feet.

"Come on. Better out than in."

As the door shut Bernadette turned to Annabel:

"Freda would be like that this morning. I had a worrying message last night and didn't sleep, and don't feel like holding her head all day. How's Lorna?"

Annabel shrugged her shoulders.

"She wouldn't say a word."

Bernadette looked sympathetic.

"Poor little cow!"

Presently Elizabeth came back.

"All is over. No flowers by request."

Annabel powdered her nose.

"Where is she?"

"She's going to the chemist as soon as she feels better. I got permission for her. I said she'd had bad news and it had upset her. I've got bad news for all of us. The Gale says there's a bride coming for a trousseau. Mrs. Pinkney's going to India and wants an outfit, and Ossy Offenbach's latest is to choose anything she likes."

Bernadette groaned.

"What a morning! I knew about the trousseau and that was bad enough. But Mrs. Pinkney! Nothing ever suits her, and as soon as you've got something off she wants 'just another peep at it.'"

Elizabeth sat on the floor to change her stockings. "Even she won't be as bad as Ossy's latest. Somebody who's never had a rag of clothes before, and pretends they've been brought up like an archduchess."

Annabel had finished changing. She lay down in her chair. "Who is Ossy Offenbach?"

Elizabeth shook her head sadly.

"Our poor dear Annabel doesn't improve. He just happens to be the richest man in England. Don't you ever read your paper?"

Bernadette settled in her chair.

"He's most frightfully generous. Supports every big charity in the country. He practically keeps the hospitals. His grandfather put every penny he could scrape into house property. I don't know how much of London Ossy owns. Most of it, I should think."

"And his reputation is bigger than his income," Elizabeth added.

Bernadette opened her paper.

"I shouldn't wonder if it's all lies. If you are as famous as he is, and as generous to all sorts of people, including girls, you are bound to get a bad reputation. Half of it is jealousy, really."

Elizabeth giggled.

"Ses you!"

Bernadette turned to the middle of her paper.

"All I know is, he's got awfully kind eyes. I bet he'd be marvellous if anyone really was in a mess."

Miss Gale hurried in.

"Now, girls. We have a very busy morning. Mr. Offenbach will be here at ten-thirty. He is bringing a niece—"

Elizabeth giggled. Miss Gale eyed her severely. "You have a very nasty mind, Elizabeth. As I was saying, he is bringing a niece. She is dark, so Annabel you will show to her, and—" She looked round, "How tiresome, isn't Freda back yet? I wanted her to show, too."

Bernadette got up.

"She won't be long. Couldn't I start?"

"Well, there's Mrs. Pinkney for you. All summer things and evening. Then I need you for the bride. She'll be in any time, and wants some tweeds. Elizabeth, you will show the wedding things. If only Freda would hurry."

Bernadette opened the door for Miss Gale.

"She won't be long, really. Don't worry, we'll manage until she comes." She shut the door, then made a face at the others. "Evidently they're all coming early. We'll never get Freda fit to show before twelve."

"Perhaps the chemist has given her something good," Annabel suggested.

Elizabeth took off her dressing-gown.

"When I last saw Freda the chemist wasn't born who could help. Raising from the dead was what she needed."

Bernadette turned to Annabel.

"You've never been here when one of us has had a black-out."

Elizabeth looked at her with unwilling gratitude.

"'One of us' is putting it nicely. Me or Freda, she means."

"It doesn't matter who," Bernadette went on quickly. "The point is we have to cover it up until she's fit to get on her feet. For if she said she was ill Miss Petoff would send for her doctor."

"Not a man you can lie to," Elizabeth, who had been seen by him, put in.

"And this time," Bernadette went on, "it would be—"

"O.U.T.," Elizabeth agreed. "Miss Petoff can't bear us girls having a binge. She says it's stupid and bad for our skins."

The showroom girls brought in the clothes. Miss Gale popped her head round the door.

"Mr. Offenbach is here; he says his niece wants every-thing, Annabel. Start with some morning things."

Annabel was just into a soft blue light wool when Freda reappeared. She said nothing, but walked slowly across to her chair and lay down. Bernadette and Elizabeth came and looked at her. They exchanged a glance. Elizabeth turned down her thumbs. Bernadette shifted a cushion from under Freda's head.

"Better keep flat. What did the chemist say?"

"Two hours," Freda answered feebly. "But I don't think I shall live as long."

Bernadette gave her a friendly pat.

"Yes, you will. Hurry up, Annabel. Now, remember, nobody is to come in here except us. One of us must always be here to take the clothes."

"That's right," agreed Elizabeth. "Don't want those nosey showroom girls talking."

"Annabel," Miss Gale's voice came through the door. Her hand was on the handle.

"Quick," Bernadette whispered. "Get out."

Annabel showed frock after frock. She had little time to think. Beyond the expected customers somebody else arrived, and it was all she and the other two could do to keep things going and not leave gaps which must at once call Miss Gale's mind to Freda. Usually she quite enjoyed her work. This morning it seemed an unutterable bore. At the back of her mind was Lorna. All very well to make excuses, but she had stolen. Might it happen again? She tried, in spite of feeling bored and worried, to help Mr. Offenbach's niece. She was a pretty little thing, but shabby. She had none of the airs and graces Elizabeth had threatened. It was easy to see the things she ought to wear. Annabel spent a shade longer on the right clothes, and tried to distract her from the wrong ones. In this she was assisted by Tania, who was tactfully giving the girl her first lesson in taste.

"There," she said at last, "two mornings. The blue and the green. That black-and-white and the brown for afternoons, and the three evening dresses, the white, the lavender and blue, and the pink. Is that right, Mr. Offenbach?"

He turned to the niece.

"Is that right?"

The girl clasped her hands. She had an attractive, husky voice.

"They're lovely."

Ossy Offenbach beckoned to Annabel.

"Come here, my child." He nodded towards the niece. "This is Miss Rose White. I saw her act at a club in Stepney, and I can tell you that one day you'll be very proud to have helped her to choose her first wardrobe. But just to mark the occasion, what about you?" He turned to Tania. "Will you see that this child chooses herself a frock? Anything she likes." He got up. "Come along, Rose."

Tania smiled at Annabel's startled face.

"Well, what is it to be?"

"Oh, please, the yellow. The one you put on the programme at the show as 'Spring Song.'"

Tania laughed.

"A very good choice. You look charming in it. I'll see it's packed for you."

In the model's room Bernadette was hurrying into a check tweed suit.

"Oh, there you are. You have been a time."

Elizabeth poked her head through the white satin slip of the frock she was putting on.

"What kept you?"

Annabel's eyes shone.

"Mr. Offenbach introduced me to that girl. Her name's Rose White, and she's to be a great actress, and because I'd helped her choose her first clothes he said I could have a frock. Any one I liked."

Until that moment it had looked as if nothing could resuscitate Freda. Now she sat up.

"Did you ever hear such lousy luck? I've walked miles and miles showing clothes to Ossy's nieces. And the first day he's feeling generous I'm too faint to show."

"Too what, dear?" Elizabeth inquired.

"Faint," said Freda firmly. "If you'd had what that chemist gave me you'd have been faint."

"Call it what you like," Bernadette interrupted, "but, thank goodness, you're better. While you've been lying there looking like a lettuce, I've shown the Pinkney 'Ladies

Tropical Outfit,' from clothes to wear at Viceregal Lodge to the last word in bathing-dresses, and I'm tired." She threw a bundle of shirts at Freda. "She wants to see all those in case she'd like them to ride in, and if she says anything about wanting 'just another peep' at one of the garments she's already seen, give her my love and say you'll show it."

Freda put her head in her hands.

"Really, Bernadette, I don't feel well enough yet."

"Any girl that has the strength to feel jealous has the strength to show." Bernadette settled down in her chair. "What did you choose, Annabel?"

Annabel sat beside her.

"The yellow. You know I've never had an evening dress."

"I wish you'd fancied white." Elizabeth struggled with a twisted sash. "I'd almost pay a bride to wear this model. It's easier to get in and out of a strait-jacket."

Freda gloomily studied her face in the glass.

"I look awful. What on earth she wants to see these shirts for, I can't think. I bet she doesn't buy them when she sees them on me." She looked at Annabel. "If you'd any decency, after getting a frock given you that ought to be mine, you'd show them."

Annabel got up.

"All right, throw one over."

Bernadette yawned.

"By the time Freda's stopped talking about herself and Annabel being the little friend of all the world the Pinkney will have gone. Step on it, one of you."

When Elizabeth and Annabel had gone to the showroom Freda mixed herself a bromo seltzer. Bernadette opened an anxious eye at the fizzing sound.

"Do you think you'd better put that on what the chemist gave you?"

Freda took a gulp.

"It's the only thing that does me good. Already I feel better." She looked thoughtfully into the cupboard. "Would you think sardines would hurt?"

Bernadette groaned.

"Of course they would, though you must have a cast-iron inside, or it would never stand the mixtures of drinks you give it. Let alone the queer meals."

Freda took a plate and the tin of sardines back to her chair. She started to open the tin.

"If," she said thoughtfully, "I had secrets to hide, I'd try and make friends with people. I wouldn't go round saying unkind things."

Bernadette watched her tip the entire tin of sardines on to her plate.

"Suspecting people have secrets is quite a different thing from knowing what they are, dear." She pointed to the plate. "If you eat all those you'll be sick again, and this time, however sick you are, you can show your own dresses."

Even when everything is wrong at home, and the one person you would like to see is in the country, nobody of Annabel's age could help being cheered by a new frock. The thought of it was in her mind as she ran down the steps of Bertna's to go out to lunch. It was so much in her mind that she missed the 'Honk, honk' of the motor horn. David stuck his head through his car window:

"Am I being cut by Miss Annabel Brown?"

"David!" A deaf mute must have felt the vibrations of gladness in Annabel's voice. David caught all that was unsaid. He gave her a rather worried smile. Then he got out of his car and opened the door:

"Will you lunch?"

They went to the Apéritif.

"The R's are almost out of the months," David said, "Let's have the last of the oysters." He ordered some white wine. Then he patted Annabel's hand under the table. "Well, am I forgiven?"

She turned crimson.

"There was nothing to forgive. I mean—"

"Oh yes, there was. If I make bad-mannered friends I ought to take the blame. But if you've really forgiven me I'll ask you something. Do you like that fellow model of yours called Bernadette something or other?"

"Yes. Why?"

"Know anything about her?"

"Nothing. What should there be to know?"

"Nothing. A friend of her's was at Eton with me. Fellow called Jim Cross. You know Cross cars. I met him hunting last week and he said something about Bertna's which made me prick up my ears. It was about Tania as a matter of fact, but one thing led to another, there was a long check and we'd time to pull the world to pieces. He said he knew this girl Bernadette. I said I knew you, and suddenly I had an idea. I asked him to get her to come to me for the week-end if I could get you. Could you manage it?"

Week-ends! Endlessly Freda and Elizabeth whispered about them. Annabel had never been away for one in her life. They had, as far as she knew, only one meaning. But a look at David convinced her that one with him must be different. He did not look quite so like a brother as sometimes, but the expression in his eyes was anything but the sort of expression Elizabeth and Freda meant. She turned pink:

"Well, I—"

Sensing she had never been invited away for a week-end before, and guessing that she might be shy, he shelved the question:

"You talk to Bernadette and let me know. It will only be the four of us. Nothing to worry about."

The oysters arrived. He poured her out a glass of wine. "How's your nice family?"

Annabel's face clouded. He should not use the word nice. Nobody called a family nice who had one of them coming up at a juvenile court for stealing. Unwillingly, she told him what had happened. Because she was sorry for Lorna, and still had a dim vision of the workings of her mind, she tried to explain how she thought it had happened. They had long ago eaten the oysters and were halfway through some 'Chicken Maryland' before she finished. David took a sip of his wine:

"Your poor mother. How's she taking it?"

"Not so badly as Dad. You see she understands us more. Besides Dad's very religious, which makes it seem worse."

David nodded:

"It shouldn't, but it does. That's why my mother found it so difficult to put up with me. How's Lorna herself?"

Annabel frowned, trying to find the words to describe just how Lorna was.

"Do you know, I don't think she quite knows why she did it. She looks terribly frightened all the time. She's so ashamed going to school because all the girls know. I asked her on Sunday why she did it, but she was crying and couldn't answer properly. But she did say she never meant to steal."

David lit a cigarette:

"Poor little devil. I expect she never did. I was at a prep. school with a kid who strangled a cat. He was expelled. I saw him for a minute before he went and he told me he had never meant to do it. He was fond of the cat. Only just at the moment it wasn't a cat it was a dragon and he was St. George."

"I don't see who Lorna could have thought she was."

"Nobody probably except herself, but I dare say she didn't mean to steal. Just a click of the brain and she'd done it."

"What worries me is she might do it again."

He shook his head:

"I bet this is a lesson to her. The trouble will be to stop her getting an inferiority complex after the case. When is it?"

"Someone's coming to see Mum to-day. But the constable said he thought Friday week."

"Friday week?" He opened his engagement book. "How about that week-end for you to come to me. You can tell me about Lorna. Perhaps I may be able to help. Will you ask Bernadette? Then if she says its all right I'll ring up Jim Cross. I'll pick you up for a drink this evening and you can let me know."

The sweet wagon was put in front of them. Annabel tried to give her attention to the vast choice on it. But there was a nervous sinking in her inside. Why was he so keen on this week-end? Why was he coming to fetch her for a drink after work, as well as giving her lunch? He had never been like that.

He hardly ever made a plan ahead, let alone all these plans in one day. Somehow she tore her mind from David to the food, and chose some fresh fruit salad. David watched her with amusement. When the waiter had poured cream on to her plate and departed, he once more patted her hand under the table.

"You're a pet, Spring Song. I went away into the country to think, and that I was very fond of you was the final result of my thinking."

Annabel picked up her spoon. She selected a slice of peach from her fruit. Sentences floated back to her. Elizabeth saying, "Everything's got to begin somewhere, and if you don't care where it ends." Bernadette's "He's differently placed. With his history he has to marry one of his own kind." Of course, she had told Bernadette that they were just friends and always would be. But then David had never said anything about being fond of her. Somehow he had changed. She looked up at him. He smiled at her. It was an amused smile.

"What is it? You have an endearing quality of looking like Alice must have looked in Wonderland when she saw the garden through the little door."

"Why do you want me to stay with you? I'm not your sort."

He made a face at her.

"Snob." Then his voice changed. "For what they'd never told me of, And what I never knew."

Annabel gazed at him blankly.

"What's that mean?"

"Ignorant child. It's from a poem. You find it and read the verse, and you'll see what it means." She looked at him with a worried, childish stare. She did not understand him in this mood. In a way it was lovely. He certainly seemed to like being with her. The way he had held her fingers made her catch her breath: and yet, if all they said was true he ought not to care. It was no good caring for people unless you could marry them. But if it came to that, what was she doing? She was caring dreadfully, so that it hurt. Yet she knew there was no thought of marriage, nor ever could be. Just suppose the same thing was by a miracle happening to David. Of course not in the same way as it was happening to her. It was natural that she should love him. It would be most unnatural that he should love her with all the girls like Octavia he could choose from. But suppose he did even a little. What then? Was the answer a week-end?

"Of course," said David, "one does not expect one's rather dull invitations jumped at, but I never before issued one which had quite such a silencing effect on the recipient."

"I'm sorry." Annabel started, and brought her thoughts back to the present. "I'll—I mean I'll ask Bernadette this afternoon, and if she says yes, then I'd like to come very much. I'm afraid I ought to go now or I'll be late."

It was nearly tea-time before Annabel managed to find herself alone with Bernadette. She was quite glad because she was dreadfully shy of giving the invitation. It looked as if she had been prying into her life, the very week after she had heard about Jim, that she should know his name, and be talking about week-ends. She did not know what to hope Bernadette would say. If she said "No" it would, of course, stop her worrying what David meant. On the other hand, if she said "Yes" it would be very exciting. It would be something to remember always if she stayed in his house.

As it happened, when she did get Bernadette to herself, she had no time to choose her words as the other two might be back any minute.

"I had lunch with David. He says he knows your Jim, and if you can come down to his house in the country the week-end after next, he'll ask him and me, too."

Bernadette stared.

"Really! I know men have a kind of masonic sign which means 'I know a girl at Bertna's, do you?' But, all the same, it's odd they connected us."

Annabel nodded, herself too confused by the curious turn of events to make any suggestions as to the workings of the male mind.

"Would you like to go?"

Bernadette smiled.

"Would a hungry man like a bit of bread? To be under the same roof as Jim is my idea of heaven. You'd like to go, wouldn't you?"

Annabel frowned.

"Awfully. More than anything I can think of. Only—"

"Only what?"

Annabel flushed.

"It's different for you. But why has he invited me?"

Bernadette grinned.

"Sleeping Beauty coming to life? The world isn't as platonic as she thought." She listened and heard steps coming down the passage. She caught hold of Annabel's hand and dropped her voice to a whisper. "You come. Any woman can refuse anything. If you've got to come to a show-down, may as well get it over. And don't forget what I told you, 'Be prepared.'"

David drove Annabel down to his place in Sussex. The English countryside on a fine day in April is perhaps lovelier than any on earth. The banks were yellow with primroses, and the hedges with catkins. There were drifts of white where the blackthorn stood. The sky was faintly blue as if it had just been washed; across it sailed some small clouds. There did not seem to be a bird but had a Te Deum to sing.

Annabel sat beside David almost choking with happiness. Saturday afternoon. They were not going back to London until early on Monday. Hours and hours of David. Even the twinge of worry as to what it all meant died, overlaid by contentment. Then there was Lorna. After so much worry the relief was grand. Of course it wasn't nice having someone coming round to see she was behaving properly, but Ethel had not minded. "It's not interference," she had said cheerfully. "Nor it doesn't mean that her mum isn't the one to look after her. But police are police, and if they let every child that took a frock off scot-free, where'd we be? No, it's right, and whatever the visitor says, Lorna'll do, or I'll know the reason why." If Annabel had a care it was George. He had been so quiet all the week, and pale; it seemed the trouble over Lorna had got him right down.

David glanced out of the corner of his eye at her serious face.

"What is it, Spring Song?"

"Nothing." She gave a blissful sigh. "I was just thinking about Dad. Funny even now the Lorna business is settled he doesn't look any better."

David sounded his horn at a cross-road.

"I'm coming down to see your parents one day soon. I think it's a mistake leaving a kid anywhere where it's made a fool of itself. Better to get her right away for a bit. I've a nice lodge-keeper and his wife who'd probably be delighted to have her for the summer."

Annabel shook her head.

"I don't expect she can go away. Somebody has to see her to know she's behaving all right."

David laughed.

"You've got a proper respect for the law, my girl, haven't you? My family never have had. I expect the matter could be arranged."

Annabel wriggled into her scat.

"Tell me about your family. Have you always lived in Sussex?"

"Not directly, but in a twisting way we always have. Mostly my relatives were a curse to their neighbours. It was forest land once, you know, and the lawless were fond of hunting somebody else's deer, and then killing their game-keepers when they argued with them."

"Did your ancestors do that?"

David nodded.

"And hanged for it, too. Then I had one very bad-tempered relative who fought duels with every other landowner for miles around, and ran two or three of them through the heart. Very unpopular he was, I believe."

Annabel could not face David belonging to such a savage lot.

"There must have been some nice ones."

"Not many. I had one, and he's not very distant either, who became a parson. He must have been a card. He collected all the likely lads of the village and taught them the trade of smuggling. He got away with it, too, because being a parson he felt he had a special right to the church, and he kept all the smuggled stuff there."

"What's the house like?"

"Elizabethan. Nearly perfect. Got a moat all round, and if you come in the summer there's a beautiful rose garden."

Annabel felt suddenly anxious. All this talk of lodge-keepers, moats and Elizabethan houses, made her feel self-conscious. Except for staying with relations, she had never been away, and then she had not gone alone. From all she had heard of David's house, it was probably enormous and full of servants, butlers and people like that.

"I expect Bernadette and Mr. Cross will be there before us," she said hopefully.

"I hope not." David slowed down the car. "I don't want anybody there when I show you the Manor for the first time. I pretend a lot, but I'm awfully proud of it, really. And round the next bend you'll see it."

Lunge Manor was a show place. That afternoon it was looking its best. David stopped the car on the crown of the hill. The house lay below them. There was a little old lodge on one side of enormous iron gates, then a wide carriage drive up to the moat across which was a bridge, then more iron gates, and then the house itself. Such renovations as had been done had been done very skilfully, and roughly the place looked as it must have looked when Queen Elizabeth came to the throne. The timber would have been beautiful then, but now, darkened and worn with weather, it made archaeologists cry. The glass in the windows was new, and so was part of the roof, but even the new parts had stood for over a hundred years.

"Oh!" Annabel gasped.

David laid his hand over hers.

"You like it?"

"Like it!" She dismissed such a silly expression. "It's the most beautiful place I have ever seen."

When Bernadette and Jim drove across the moat neither David nor Annabel was in sight.

"They're here," said Bernadette, pointing to the car. "Better ring."

The butler who appeared told them that he believed his Lordship had taken Miss Brown up into the wood. He had said that when they arrived he was to order tea and sound a gong. There was something in the way the butler spoke that made Bernadette certain that a lot of gongs had been beaten to bring young David into meals.

"Does he always obey gongs?"

The butler took her case. A faint smile was hinted at the corner of his lips.

"Always, miss. Her Ladyship, his Lordship's mother, that is, was never one to bear with unpunctuality at the table."

Shown their rooms, Jim and Bernadette hung out of their respective bedroom windows and laughed to see the butler cross the lawn and stand at the top of a flight of steps solemnly beating a loud-voiced gong.

"All right, Elliot," came David's voice. "We've heard." He and Annabel came down the garden.

Of course the cherry was in flower, the daffodils opening, that heart-catching spring scent in the air. But did that account for the radiance that surrounded the two? Bernadette caught her breath. If ever she was to see happiness it was now. She looked across at Jim's window. He felt the glance and turned to her. He had evidently seen what she had seen, but to him it was personal. There was bitterness and suffering in his eyes. She turned back into her room. She felt as though a cloud had crossed the sun. She shivered and went over to the log fire. Poor Jim! If only she had the courage to tell him. He would, of course, never see her again. But wouldn't he be happier? She believed he would. Queer that love such as she had to give was not sufficiently selfless to set him free.

Annabel, looking back on the week-end, found it hard to remember what she had done with the hours. There was dinner in the lovely banqueting hall at a great polished table, though there was electric light, it was lit with candles. Afterwards they had inspected the big guest-room where, like every other of the period, Queen Elizabeth was supposed to have spent a night.

"The poor old girl can never have had a night at home," David said, "and I for one always deny she ever came here. I like to think the night she might have come here was one of her nights off. But I'll tell you who did sleep here and is supposed to sleep here still. My great-great-great-grandmother who was said to be a witch."

Bernadette was enchanted.

"What sort of witchery?"

"The worst kind of magic. She talked to the devil. And in this very room." He lowered his voice to a suitable melodrama hush, "And even now, so they say, whenever the wind is high the devil gets blown in at the window and here he meets great-great-great-Granny."

"Really?" Annabel's eyes were round. "Aren't you afraid to sleep in the house? Did you ever see her or him?"

"Him," David corrected, "is a very saucy way of speaking of the devil. No, I never did. But hereabouts, whenever there is a storm, the farmers say, 'Proper visiting night it was,' and that's what they mean."

They had left the ghost and opened the drawing-room window. David said that they had all got to hear the nightingales. But they only heard a couple of owls having an argument.

Later they had played a silly card game, and then there had been bed.

Sunday had been an equally lovely day. David said he had to go to church when he was home, but he never expected his guests to go. However they all went and were disturbed in the middle of the sermon by Jim leaning across Bernadette to whisper to David.

"Where did the smuggling parson keep the stuff?"

In the afternoon Jim and Bernadette had gone one way and David and Annabel another. David and Annabel went to inquire after a farmer who was ill. David went inside and talked to the sick man while Annabel helped the farmer's wife stir a disgusting mess for the pigs. They meant to walk sedately home after that, but instead they found a stream in the wood and David started to explain theoretically how streams were dammed. After a bit his lesson stopped being theoretical and became practical. Presently they were both splashing stones into the water. They got in a horrible mess.

In the evening they sat round a big fire and talked, and argued whether it was better to be bored by advertisements from Luxembourg or to be being educated by the B.B.C. They laughed a lot, and sometimes Jim managed to get the B.B.C. heard and sometimes David, Luxembourg. It was in a B.B.C. period that the news came through.

"There is an S.O.S. Will the daughter of Henry Milton Aston go to him at once as he is seriously ill."

"Henry Milton Aston." Jim's tone was bitter. "I hope he dies."

"Funny not to tell the daughter where to go to," said Annabel, "they always do."

Bernadette got up. Her face was grey. She fixed her eyes on Jim.

"This time there's no need. He's in Wormwood Scrubs, and his daughter's going to him."

Chapter Ten

Annabel and David stood on the steps and watched Jim and Bernadette drive away. As the car disappeared across the moat Annabel turned to David.

"What did her father go to prison for?"

David took her arm and led her back into the house.

"Share conversion and fraud. He got fifteen years." He calculated a moment. "Must have done close on five of them."

"Well then, Bernadette was still at school when he did it. She couldn't have known anything about it. It was silly of her not to tell Jim, but I expect she thought he'd mind about her father being in prison."

"It wasn't that, poor kid! Naturally nobody hankers to have a pa-in-law lolling in Wormwood Scrubs, though I suppose one would get accustomed to it. But, you see, the Crosses were mixed up in the scandal."

"What, Jim?"

"No, old Fred Cross, his father. He was a big name in the city, put him on the directorate and he established confidence. He believed in Henry Aston. When the crash came he not only lost every penny of his own money, but dozens who had trusted him lost everything. Many of them the savings of a lifetime. He couldn't stand it. He shot himself."

"Goodness, how awful! And it was Bernadette's father's fault. Of course he couldn't marry her."

David lit a cigarette.

"I doubt if you're as fond of anyone as old Jim is of that girl you'd let anything stand in the way of your happiness. After all, what's the good of mucking up a second generation because of the mistakes of the first. Besides, he has done the needful towards his father. He and his brother are paying back the shareholders. It's a good show, for it's costing them a hell of a lot, and there was no reason why they should worry."

It seemed to Annabel in that moment that Bernadette's happiness was the one thing that mattered. The week-end had been so perfect it would be nice if there were a permanent memorial to it.

"Oh, dear, I do hope they marry."

David laughed at her anxious tone.

"So do I. While they're packing our suit-cases we'll try and help, we'll—"

"Are we going?" Annabel interrupted.

"My sweet," he put his arms round her shoulders, "think of the proprieties. Elliot is a very respectable man; I expect he'd stop butlering us if he thought we'd spent a night here unchaperoned."

"Of course, how stupid of me." Annabel flushed. What must he think of her? A girl like Octavia would probably have insisted on leaving at the same time as Bernadette.

But David was not apparently thinking any more about the subject. He called out to Elliot to hurry the servants over the packing, then he pulled Annabel into the dining-room.

"Come along. We'll offer a bribe to my great-great-great-granny. In the village they say she has remarkable powers still. I'm told, though I've never tried it myself, that she's still fond of a drink, and if one is left out for her she's prepared to be helpful."

"What sort of a drink?"

"I've no idea. You choose." He pointed to the decanters. "Here we have brandy, whisky, sherry, port and gin. But for Jim's and Bernadette's happiness I'm prepared to go further. If you think it'll please the old lady we'll have up a bottle of champagne."

Annabel giggled.

"Aren't you silly?"

"Not a bit. Use your wits, girl. What tipple do witches prefer?"

Annabel considered the decanters.

"I think port."

"Right." David poured out a glass. "Come along." He led the way up to the big bedroom.

The room was eerie in the dusk. There were deep shadows under the bed canopy and shadows where the furniture stood against the wall.

Annabel clutched David's arm.

"It does seem as if she really might come."

David lowered his voice to a sinister whisper.

"She will."

"Shall I turn on the light?" Annabel suggested.

"The light!" David's tone was shocked. "Witches hate lights." He crossed to the window. "We'll put it on the ledge, and one night soon, when the wind is high, it can blow in great-great-great-Grandmamma and—"

"And give us our wish."

There was a funny hush as Annabel finished speaking. Both she and David stood staring at the dim outline of the glass of port. David broke the silence.

"I wonder if the old lady's idea about what we were wishing and ours quite coincide."

Annabel started. "What we were wishing." She had forgotten why they were there. Her wish had run, "Let him always like me."

There were steps outside. David took her hand.

"Come on, serious one. That's our luggage going down."

It was after eight before David and Annabel reached London. They had driven up almost in silence. Not the silence of people who are short of things to say, but the silence of friends who don't need to say they like being together. As they crossed the river David switched on the light under his clock.

"Look at the time. I'm ravenous, are you? We'll nip into the Carlton Grill and ask Charles to give us a quick bite, and then I'll drive you home." Charles found them a table with more than his Maitre d'Hotel pleasure; he was sincerely glad to see David and delighted he was with such a pretty girl. David looked up at him and grinned.

"We're in a hurry. On the other hand, we think nothing quite good enough for us. Suppose you choose a meal?"

The meal was short and perfect, but Charles and the wine waiter (who looked like a bishop) exchanged understanding smiles. It was clear that neither the food, nor the really exquisite wine, meant anything to the two they were serving. David and Annabel could think only of each other. Their talk was banal. David wanted to know if she had liked his house. She wanted stories of when he was a child. It was when, with untasting palates, they were swallowing "Crepes Suzette" that David said:

"Darling, before I drive you home, I want you to come to my flat. I've something to show you."

Annabel gazed at her plate. The room swam. So it had come as they all said it must. The ghosts of dead conversations hung round her chair. "When the evening comes you are asked to go back to the flat—" "It's a hang-over from the Naughty Nineties. . . . I think they hope we aren't fussy, to put it mildly." "'No' would probably mean saying 'good-bye.'" "Any woman can refuse anything. If you've got to come to a show-down, may as well get it over." Words, words, words. So easy to talk. It wasn't true it was better to get things over. Getting things over meant finishing them. It meant saying "Good-bye, David." And when that was said it would be like living in a fog, thick greyness everywhere, and nothing to hold on to. At least she could give herself a little more happiness. It needn't be to-night. She looked up.

"I think I ought to get straight on. They'll be in bed if I don't hurry."

David was paying the bill. He spoke without looking up from the change he was sorting.

"I shan't keep you long." He got up. The waiter moved the table for them. "Come on. Be a good girl and don't argue."

David's flat was in Mount Street. The streets had a Sunday clearness of traffic. To Annabel they seemed to be going at seventy miles an hour. She clasped her hands. Her heart throbbed so loudly, she wondered David could not hear it. There was no doubt in her mind what she had to say. The difficulty was to bring herself to say it. David stopped the car.

"Well, here we are."

Annabel crushed her fingers so tightly into each other she momentarily stopped their circulation.

"I—I'm sorry, but I can't."

He got out of the driver's seat and opened the door on her side.

"Can't what? Come on. All day I've wanted to say some-thing—"

"I know." She nodded. "I've guessed you did. I know I've probably let you think I'm like that, but I'm not."

He stared at her.

"What are you talking about?" He took her by the arm and pulled her out of the car. The street lamp shone on her face. "What are you suggesting?"

"I'm not," Annabel stammered, searching for words. "I mean I thought that was what you meant."

There was a frightful pause. All the amusement went out of David's face, he looked bitter. He dropped her arm.

"You cheap-minded little idiot! Do you think all the world's like the worst film? You, of all people, with a decent home and decent background. You don't know what you've killed to-night. When I met you it was as if I'd come out of a greenhouse stuffed with a lot of queer-looking orchids into a field of cowslips. I thought you were simple and honest, and that through your eyes it would be possible to get back to liking simple things. But I was wrong. You've got a dirty, cheap little mind, and I was a fool to think anything else." He held up his hand and stopped a passing taxi. He took Annabel's suitcase from Iris car and put it beside the driver. He opened the door and handed her in. Then he gave the driver a note.

"Take this lady to 110, Mercia Lane, Coulsden."

It sometimes seemed to Ethel that life just had to go badly. Sunday night she went to bed almost happy for the first time for days. Of course they were not out of the wood with Lorna. The child looked ill and wretched, and shame seemed to have made her bitter. She would not see any of her friends, and after school hung about the house moping. At the Court they had suggested that she should join a troop of girl guides, or go to evening drill classes. Ethel considered they had been very kind and understanding at the children's court, and, if the magistrate thought guides or something of that sort the right thing for Lorna, she was willing she should join. But in her own mind she scoffed at the idea. It wasn't guides or drill Lorna needed, it was to get right away where every time she left the house she did not have to imagine people saying, "There's Lorna Brown who stole a dress." All the same, things for Lorna might have gone a lot worse, and Ethel was thankful.

Then it was nice to feel Annabel was having her week-end in the country. In the ordinary way Ethel would have been worried sick by that week-end. Then she had heard that nice Miss Lord was going, too. One look and Ethel had known there was nothing fishy about Bernadette. Obviously she was not brought up to the world in which she was now working, but she was not one to take a girl on a visit that had anything queer about it. Ethel wished Annabel were not so palpably in love. Lord de Bett was not her sort, and he was not to blame for not seeing how Annabel felt about him. Likely as not, half the young women in London were after him, and naturally he could not be expected to notice how a girl like Annabel was feeling. Still, it was nice she was having her week-end in the country. When the time came and he was not paying any more attention to her, and she was settling down to marry some nice boy of her own sort, that visit would be something to look back on. Provided you had nothing to be ashamed of, Ethel did not think a woman could have too much to look back on. Over sewing or washing-up it was nice to have something to smile over, if it was only a memory.

"There," she said to George as she got into bed, "no big worries now, we ought to sleep easy."

George was not yet in bed. He sat on the side of it.

"Ethel, old girl, I haven't said anything because we had our other trouble, but now that's fixed, I've got a bit of bad news."

Ethel, in one of those quick mind flashes, faced a drop in wages at Fordwych's, finished for the present with her green velvet curtains, and cut down their necessary summer wardrobe by half. When she looked at George she had taken the blow and was able to smile.

"Fordwych's struck another bad patch?"

"No." George licked his lips.

Ethel looked at him with a sudden clutch of fear.

"What is it, old dear?"

George fiddled with a button of his pyjamas.

"The Monday after Lorna had her trouble I had to go to the doctor's."

"Why?"

"You know I'd been having a bit of indigestion. Well, that morning I was taken bad. I thought it was just being upset over Lorna, but the doctor thought differently. He sent me to hospital for an X-ray. They want to operate."

Ethel caught the carefully controlled panic behind the quiet statement. She had a horror of operations, but this was no moment to voice it.

"What does the doctor say is the matter?" Her voice was so unworried that George sucked in a ray of comfort.

"There's a tumour. It may be nothing, but you never know with them. He said that himself."

"Did he?" Ethel sounded as if had she only had the doctor there she would have wrung his neck for frightening her husband. "Well, most of the tumours I've known were tumours and no more."

George shook his head.

"I've a premonition, Ethel. I think it's finish for me."

Ethel was shocked. Things might be bad, but the word "finish" could not be used in her hearing. She put her arm round George's shoulder. Her hug was as reassuring as those she gave Maudie when she was scared in the dark.

"Old fuss-pot, aren't you? Always were. But I can think of a night when it wasn't you that did the fussing. It was the night before Maudie was born. Do you remember?"

George pulled his mind from his own troubles for a moment.

"You were in a taking."

"That's right, made a proper fool of myself. Sat down and cried and told you I was going to die. Do you know what you said?"

"No."

"You said, 'Time enough to cry when the milk jug's smashed. No good getting upset while the milk's still in the jug.'"

"Did I?" George was impressed by this pearl of common sense which had fallen from his lips.

"You did, and it wouldn't do any harm for you to remember it now. You come into bed and keep warm. It won't help that tumour if you have pneumonia."

George lay down. Ethel thought his face looked very grey against the pillow. She slipped her fingers into his.

"I'm glad my life insurance is paid right up," George said. "In time Alfie will be working and he's a good boy and will help. Then there's Annabel. She'll be willing to give a bit more. Maybe when the time comes she could get Lorna into the same business. Might keep Lorna straight working with Annabel. I should keep up the payments on the house. It's an investment and—"

"Now look here," Ethel broke in, "we haven't buried you yet, and I'm not expecting to. So let's finish with all this talk. Which day do they want to operate?"

"I'm to go in Wednesday." George sighed, "Foolish of me to think of it, but I wish it was any other hospital. That's where they took Charlie Pink, our Midlands traveller. Of course, I knew it was about hopeless before he went in, but you know how it is."

"Of course it's silly, but I'd feel the same myself." Ethel ran her mind over her slight knowledge of hospitals. "There's plenty of hospitals about. Do you have to go to that one?"

"Yes. I asked the doctor. Seem it's difficult for him to get me a bed in one of the others." He squeezed Ethel's fingers, finding comfort in speaking clearly of his fears. "I'd feel a lot easier if it could be done somewhere else."

Ethel murmured soothing agreement, but her mind was hard at work ferreting round for help. Who did they know who might know someone at a hospital? There was the vicar, he was worth trying. Then there was Mr. Fordwych and his son, but George would have to speak to them, and he could never bring himself to ask a favour. It was at this point she heard the taxi stop. She sat up:

"That's at our door." She got out of bed and went to the window and moved the curtain so that she could see the gate. She came hurrying back and pulled on her dressing-gown. "It's Annabel. I suppose they had to get back to-night on account of their work. I'll go down and let her in."

Ethel hurried to the hall, her heart suddenly lighter. Annabel was home. She could tell her about George. It would be a wonderful help to tell the story, instead of having to hear it and make light of it. Then there was another thing. Annabel could help. It was silly of her not to have thought of it at once. Who could be more likely to know someone at a hospital than a peer? Annabel should ask Lord de Bett.

On the long taxi drive to Coulsden, Annabel sat in the corner of the taxi scarcely moving. She who had cried so easily all her life had met something which hurt so much it stopped the tears from coming. "You cheap-minded little idiot." Over and over again, the words repeated in her brain. They kept pace with the purr of the engine. "Cheap-minded little idiot. Cheap-minded little idiot."

Annabel's cheeks burned. How could she have been such a fool? To listen to the gossip of two girls who didn't know him, and the warnings of Bernadette before she had met him. In the past enchanting hours she had not troubled to ask Bernadette what she felt. But why had she to ask Bernadette, or listen to chatter? Why had she not trusted her own instinct which had always been right about him? There was no excuse for her. She had known him when he treated her as an elder brother and she had felt the change when he had come back to town with the added warmth in his friendship. What had she lost? What had he meant?—"It was as if I'd come out of a green-house stuffed with queer orchids, into a field of cowslips." It was clear enough what he meant when he said "I thought you were simple and honest, and that through your eyes it would be possible to get back to liking simple things." "Through your eyes"! Then he had meant to go on seeing her. "Through your eyes." It was unbelievable, but could he have meant to ask her to marry him? It didn't matter. Nothing mattered now. With one cheap common remark she had killed her happiness as she might have squashed a slug with her foot. She had only one wish. To get home to Mum. Nothing could help.

But she would tell Mum and in sharing what she had done there would be relief.

Ethel opened the door.

"Well dear, this is a surprise." She took the suit-case. "Come in. I'll put on the electric fire and make you a cup of something." She tucked her arm into Annabel's: "My word, I'm glad to see you. I've got something to tell you. What'll you have?"

"Nothing."

"Well come and sit down a minute." Ethel drew her unprotesting into the sitting-room and pushed her into one of the armchairs. She knelt down and connected the electric fire. Then she settled in the other chair.

"Dad's got a tumour."

"A tumour!" The words penetrated even through Annabel's self-absorbing misery.

"Yes." Away from George Ethel faced the truth. "That may mean cancer, or it may be just something that's got to come away and he'll be right as rain in a week or two."

"Poor Dad! I wish I could help."

"Well you can." Ethel drew her chair forward. "There's a chap that works at Fordwych's went into the hospital not long ago pretty near dying. They operated, but he died. Well Dad can't seem to fancy going to the same hospital. I want you to see if you can get him into another."

"Me! How?"

"Ask Lord de Bett."

Annabel looked across at her mother. Queer that at a time when it seemed she could feel nothing but her own suffering she should see Ethel so clearly.

The hands folded tightly together lying on the knees of her red dressing-gown. Many times she had noticed in a vague way what nicely shaped hands Ethel had, but it was only to-night that she noticed that they were rough with work and at the same time what an effort had been made to keep them nice. Ethel slept with her hair in a plait. Annabel had often seen that plait, but it was only to-night it linked up with wretched nights when she had been coughing or feverish and the door had opened and there had been the shadow of a hand carefully screening a candle, then Ethel leaning over the bed with that plait over her shoulder. Then those eyes. Ethel's eyes were an unusual blue, clear like a bird's-eye, and the colour was not fading as she grew older. Annabel had seen those eyes with almost every expression, but never till to-day had she seen them pleading. Odd to have Mum begging for something, it seemed to alter their positions. Till that moment Annabel had not really considered herself grown-up where Mum was concerned. She had come home not meaning to be grown-up at all, but to behave childishly. No one could comfort, but it would have been good to have Mum to cling to in the darkness around her. But now she knew even that help was denied her. For years Mum had been propping them all up, now it was she who needed help, and she was expecting Annabel to give it.

Ethel's expression had changed.

"What is it, Annabel? You will ask him, won't you? He's the only one we know who could help, and I can't have Dad in a hospital he's afraid of."

Annabel got up. Somehow she managed a confident smile.

"You won't have to, Mum." She drew her mother to her feet. "Come along to bed. Don't worry, I'll have everything fixed to-morrow, you'll see."

"There," Ethel beamed through tear-clouded eyes, "I knew you would. I'll go up and tell Dad. Maybe it'll make him sleep." Suddenly she noticed Annabel's face. "Bless me child, what's the matter with you? You're as white as a sheet."

Annabel stooped and put out the fire.

"Nothing. I was a bit car-sick, that's all."

"Had a good time?"

"Lovely."

"That's good," Ethel kissed her, "then goodnight dear. I must go to Dad, you've taken a real load off my mind, God bless you."

Annabel shut the bedroom door. She did not turn on the light for fear of waking Lorna. Mechanically she dragged off her things. In bed she lay rigid. Then suddenly she began to shake as if she had an ague. Dry sobs choked her. She turned her face into her pillow to smother their sound. David gone. Dad ill, perhaps going to die. Worst of all, Mum depending on a promise she could not possibly keep. "Ask David"! She stuffed the sheet in her mouth to stop herself screaming. "Ask David." Dear God if only she could.

Ethel, because she had to have an excuse to fuss over him, kept George in bed for breakfast.

"If Fordwych's have started your sick leave from to-day," she explained, "then I'm starting to make an invalid of you from to-day. Anyway, old dear, what's the matter with reading your paper comfortably in bed instead of crushed into that train?"

Of course bringing up a breakfast tray was not enough. Ethel had to sit on the edge of the bed while he ate. She read funny bits out of the paper and took his attention so that he ate quite a decent meal. She was shocked to find what poor self-control she had. Twice while she was reading a lump came into her throat so that she could hardly get the words out, and she had to pass it off by pretending she was laughing.

If Ethel had been downstairs for breakfast she could not have failed to be struck by how ill Annabel looked. She had been awake most of the night, and had finally dropped into an unpleasant two hours of nightmare-haunted sleep, from which she woke with a start to a depression which made her heavy and dull and mercifully almost incapable of coherent thought.

Breakfast was no help. With Ethel upstairs she had to give some attention to the children and their questions almost made her scream. Alfie at once felt something was wrong.

"Why's Dad having his breakfast in bed?"

"He isn't very well."

"What's the matter with him?"

"Nothing much."

"Is the doctor coming?"

"I think so."

Then Lorna had her piercing eye on her sister.

"My goodness, what did you do while you were . . . away? You look simply awful. Doesn't she, Alfie?"

Alfie took his mind off his father and studied Annabel.

"Gosh! Are you going to be sick? You look as if you might be going to be."

Annabel managed a light tone:

"Sillies. I'm all right. As a matter of fact I was a bit car-sick coming back last night."

Alfie and Lorna looked horrified.

"What in the car?" Alfie asked.

Lorna thought of David.

"How awful for Lord de Bett. I'm sure the sort of girls he usually goes with, those like Miss Glaye, aren't sick in cars."

"I wasn't sick in the car." Annabel explained wearily.

"Then where was you sick?" Maudie enquired.

"Nowhere." Annabel got up. "Now I've got to go to catch my train."

Lorna looked at the clock.

"You're starting ten minutes earlier than you usually do. Why?"

Annabel just succeeded in keeping her temper.

"Because I want to. Now finish your breakfasts quietly and don't disturb Dad."

There was a letter for Annabel when she reached Bertna's. For one intoxicating moment, while she only realised there was a letter, and had not seen the writing, she thought it was from David, but a glance showed her Bernadette's unmistakable scrawl.

Dear Annabel,

I am writing this to catch the midnight post. Father died just after I got to the prison hospital. I can't be sorry. When he saw me he smiled almost like he used to before it all happened. He said "Hullo, Duckie, I'm just off. God is a more generous judge than the one down here. He thinks fifteen years too long." He became unconscious soon after that and never said any more. Jim's been an angel. I expect David told you about me after we had gone. Of course, it's no good pretending Jim wouldn't rather I was somebody else's daughter, but all the same he seems to feel that I'm me no matter what our parents did. Anyway, as soon as possible, we are sneaking off somewhere out of range of the reporters' cameras to be married by special licence.

I am ringing up Tania to tell her that I'm not coming back. She has always known me and will understand.

As far as the rest of Bertna's are concerned, I'd like my disappearance to be wrapped in mystery, but this may not be possible as when I arrived at the prison last night it was surrounded by cameras. I covered my face, but certainly some of them got a snap before I realised they were there. If those sweet little dears, Freda and Elizabeth, should see a picture and ask questions, act the village idiot and know nothing.

If that broadcast had not come when it did I had something to say to you. I think I've been unnecessarily fussy on your behalf. If ever I saw a man in love David is. I'll hope to read of your engagement, and some day the Crosses will entertain the de Betts.

Bless you. Even at a moment when I should be unhappy, I can see we are two very lucky people. I find it odd anyone as heavenly as him can be fond of me. Do you feel like that about David?

Bernadette.

Annabel was the first to arrive. She was glad. Her self-control was not proof against a letter like that. "If ever I saw a man in love David is." "I find it odd anyone as heavenly as Jim can be fond of me. Do you feel like that about David?" Did she? Annabel dared not cry. She stood in the middle of the room, with her eyes shut, her hands gripping her throat. It ached as if it had a disease.

"David," she whispered, "David."

Freda and Elizabeth arrived together. Freda held out a picture paper.

"Well! To think who we've been mixing with. Have you seen?"

Annabel examined the paper. There was no doubt it was Bernadette. The camera had evidently caught her unawares. Her eyes were startled and her hand was on her scarf preparatory to covering her face. The caption said "Affecting bedside scene. Aston's daughter comes to say good-bye to her father."

Annabel kept looking at the paper while she tried to think of something to say which would not show that she knew. An expression of the children's came to her:

"Gosh!"

Freda snatched back the paper. She looked at Elizabeth.

"I think our dear Annabel knew we were housing the gaolbird's daughter."

Annabel lost her temper.

"If her father was in prison it wasn't her fault."

"No," Elizabeth agreed, "but I think we ought to have known. One could have locked up one's purse."

Annabel saw red.

"You beast. How can you talk like that. You know she wasn't a bit like that. She was the only person who was nice here. Now it'll be awful and—"

Freda came over to her and caught her arm:

"Then you did know. Isn't she coming back?"

"I don't know. I mean—"

Annabel was spared further prevarication by the arrival of Miss Bell.

"Hurry up, girls. Annabel, that young lady, Miss Rose White, who Mr. Offenbach brought the other day, will be in for another day dress. You can start by showing the new grey."

Annabel, assisted by Miss Bell, put on the frock. She went to the glass to do her hair. She was shocked at her face. Lines half down her cheeks and not a bit of colour. Miss Bell smiled sourly.

"Your face isn't looking its best, is it? However, I suppose if you girls choose to keep late hours, poor Miss Petoff has to suffer. Now run along down."

As the door closed behind Miss Bell and Annabel, Elizabeth gave a puzzled look at Freda.

"What's it matter if Annabel knew about Bernadette, or not? At least, it looks as if Bernadette wouldn't come back, so why worry?"

Freda fingered her paper, smiling to herself. She had the greatest respect for Elizabeth's looks and sex-appeal, but none at all for her wits, which she knew to be non-existent. It was a comfort, for otherwise she, too, might realise that it could be worth money to know somebody who was news.

Down in the showroom Rose White was sitting beside Miss Gale; she smiled cheerfully at Annabel.

"Good morning." She looked at the dress Annabel was wearing. "I'm not sure that's what I want. Mr. Offenbach has got me a job. Isn't it exciting? I start rehearsals next week." She looked pleadingly at Annabel. "What do you think I ought to wear at a rehearsal?"

Annabel looked as blank as she felt.

"I don't know. Something darker, do you think, that won't show the dirt?"

Rose nodded.

"That's what I thought. Have you anything like that?"

Annabel was conscious that Rose was like herself. She was fumbling about in a strange world, not certain what to wear, or what to do. She was afraid of making mistakes, just as she had been herself. At the thought her eyes filled with tears.

"I'll go and see," she muttered, and ran out of the room.

Miss Gale had gone when Annabel returned. Rose beckoned her over to her.

"She's gone to telephone," she whispered. She fingered the navy woollen Annabel was wearing. "Do you think it will stretch?"

"No." Annabel turned up the skirt to show it was backed. "I should say it was just the thing. Would you like to slip it on, or shall I show you some others?"

"I'll try it on." Rose gave her a friendly smile. "What did you choose?"

"Choose?" Annabel queried stupidly.

"The frock Uncle Ossy said you could have."

"Oh, that. I chose the yellow evening dress."

"What is it?" Rose's husky voice was full of sympathy. She laid her hand on Annabel's sleeve.

"Nothing." Annabel tried to pull away.

"But, there is. Come on, perhaps I could help. Or, if I couldn't, I could ask Uncle Ossy. You've no idea how kind he is."

Uncle Ossy! A conversation suddenly came back to Annabel. "He's frightfully generous. Practically keeps the hospitals." She looked with sudden hope at Rose. Her promise to Ethel. She couldn't keep it, she couldn't ask David for anything. But if Mr. Offenbach would help, wouldn't that be better?

"It's my father. He's got to have an operation. He doesn't like the hospital he's going into, do you think—"

Rose nodded.

"Here's the assistant coming back."

Even in her present upset state, Annabel noticed the word "assistant," and thought how Miss Gale would have writhed if she had heard it.

"He's away to-day," Rose went on, "but I'll tell him, it'll be all right, don't worry."

Freda was in a bad temper. It seemed the press already knew that Bernadette had been a model at Bertna's. What they were interested in was Freda's veiled hints about a romance. And that was what annoyed her. She had nothing but the vaguest hints to give. For a good story, and the present address of Miss Aston, she was told she could have quite a nice sum of money. It infuriated her to think that there was a nice sum of money so nearly hers, and she unable to claim it. She blamed Annabel. She was certain Annabel could help if she would. She said to her:

"I wonder where Bernadette is. I should like to write to her about her father."

But Annabel only replied: "I wonder."

Later Freda suggested:

"I think us girls ought to send a wreath to Bernadette's father's funeral. I shall ask Miss Petoff for her address."

But when she did ask Tania all she got was:

"Ring up the prison; I expect they'll know where the funeral is going to be."

She packed all Bernadette's belongings into a box and went with a sweet smile to Miss Gale. "These are Bernadette's. Do you know her address? I thought I ought to forward them, she might be wanting them."

"No, I don't," snapped Miss Gale, "and I wish you'd mind your own business."

Freda was very hurt. By this time she had persuaded herself that sheer kindness of heart was causing her search. She took the box to Miss Bell.

"This wants forwarding to Bernadette. I asked Miss Gale for the address, and she said she'd forgotten it. But I knew you would know. You never forget anything."

Miss Bell gave what the girls called "her old-fashioned look."

"I never met such a Paul Pry as you are, Freda," she said acidly.

"Well," thought Freda, "there's only one thing for it. I must watch Annabel. I expect she'll go and see her."

All Monday Freda kept her eyes glued, but Annabel was disappointing. She looked wretched and hardly spoke, remained in for lunch and, at the end of the day, hurried off to the station and caught her train to Coulsden. Freda thought that Tuesday was going to be as bad, but at about twelve Annabel was told she was wanted on the telephone. Try as she would, Freda could not get much out of it. She hid behind the curtain in the passage where the 'phone was, but by the time she got there the conversation was nearly over.

"Thank you," said Annabel. "Yes. Six o'clock." She put down the receiver, and went back to the models' room.

Freda came out from her hiding-place, scowling.

"Aren't people inconsiderate? Six o'clock. That puts paid to my cocktail party."

Annabel asked if she might leave ten minutes early. Freda could not very well make the same request, so she left without asking. Annabel took a taxi. Freda, with a frown, for she hated waste, took another. Annabel's taxi turned north.

"Follow it," said Freda.

Annabel went to a house in Chester Terrace, Regents Park. Freda stopped her taxi at the end of the private road.

"We'll keep on the Park side. Don't want it known we are following."

Annabel rang the bell at a house gay with window boxes. A Rolls Royce stood at the door.

"A Rolls!" thought Freda. "That belongs to Bernadette's man." She got out of the taxi and paid the driver. Then she took up a strategic position where, through the shrubbery, she could see all that went on.

Freda had waited about half an hour when the front door opened again. She leant forward. She let out a low whistle. On the step stood Ossy Offenbach. He led Annabel to his car.

"Dawson will drive you home. Now, my dear, you're not to worry, you'll telephone me on Thursday. I'm sure I shall hear it's an occasion for a little celebration."

Freda stared after the car. David de Bett and now Ossy Offenbach. Well, well! It was disappointing not to find out about Bernadette, but the evening hadn't been wasted. Octavia would pay. She stopped a passing taxi.

"Drive me to the nearest telephone box."

CHAPTER ELEVEN

IT IS all very well to lose your temper overnight, but it's quite another thing to remain angry the next morning, especially if you are fond of the person you were angry with. David woke in the early hours of Monday morning wishing he had not said the things he had said as unkindly as he had said them. Annabel had been so enchanting over the week-end. She had been even more endearingly Alice in Wonderland than he had ever seen her. She had adored Lunge, not the kind of adoring that has to exclaim all the time, but the sort that breathes in atmosphere until the adored is part of themselves. She had so obviously loved Lunge, and Lunge loved her, that he had known he was right. If Annabel would marry him he would be happy and he believed he could make her happy. It was perhaps silly of him to have planned to ask her in that way, but how was he to know she thought those sort of things about him? In the early hours it is easy to let your imagination run away with you. David writhed. Had it all been lies? Wasn't Annabel the simple little thing she had always pretended to be? Was all her talk of never having been about before a sham? Had other men made love to her? At that hour it seemed the only explanation. How otherwise could she have so misread him? He went over in his mind every meeting with her. Had he even by a glance given her a reason for getting him so wrong? He was sure he hadn't. All the same, he wished he hadn't said quite those things. She had looked so white in the lamplight. Her eyes so horribly hurt. A clock struck four. With a curse he got out of bed. Blast it, why had she treated him like that? Why? Why? He lit a cigarette and pulled back the curtains, and looked down into the street. Only so few hours ago and he had been so damned happy. Stupid sort of bloke, he supposed he was, to count on luck before he got it. Then suddenly he threw away his cigarette, and turned on a bath. He wasn't going to stay moping here. He'd go to Lunge.

Some houses have the power of soothing. Lunge Manor was like that. It was almost impossible in Lunge to have those sort of nagging discussions with yourself that consist in going over and over past conversations, thinking of better answers that should have been made. There was nothing trivial about the place, and it had a way of sweeping pettiness out of people. David had never been a person to churn thoughts over in his mind. He usually liked people, and expected them to like him; if they did not he neither knew nor cared. This was the first time he had even considered what impression he was making, and his first flight into introspection made him ashamed.

Even as his car crossed the moat he began to wonder if he could have misjudged Annabel. By the next morning he was sure he had, and by Tuesday night he could not wait another minute without telling her so.

"Elliott," he said, "I'm going back to town to-morrow."

But the morning brought a letter.

My dear David,

I rang your flat last flight and heard you'd gone to Lunge. Don't think I'm trying to reopen our friendship. I know you thought I was a beast that Sunday, and I expect I was. I've been awfully ashamed of myself since. But yesterday I heard something which comforted me a tiny bit. That little Annabel of yours isn't any good. She's taken on Ossy Offenbach. A friend of mine who knows told me.

I'm afraid it's a case. Apparently he's quite open about it.

*I do feel sorry to have to write this, for one does
so hate hurting one's pals' friendships, but I should
never have forgiven myself if I hadn't let you know.
If ever you're passing, drop in and have a drink.
Yours,
Octavia.*

*

Ethel and Annabel sat together in the kitchen drinking cocoa.

"Wonderful," said Ethel, "what these high-up people can do. Fancy, all fixed on the telephone!"

Annabel nodded.

"You wouldn't believe how easy it all seemed. He just heard what the Doctor said was wrong with dad, and what it might be, and then he said: 'Tommy's the best man for that operation. I forget which hospital is his, but we'll soon find out.' Then he rang up the man he called Tommy and explained everything, and asked for our doctor's name and address, and then he put down the receiver and he said to me, "They'll take your father in at St. Thomas's to-morrow, and my friend'll operate the next morning."

"Wonderful!" Ethel stirred her cocoa. "It's made a lot of difference to Dad. Even if it's bad news he feels everything that can be done has been done."

"Mum!" Annabel got off her chair and knelt at Ethel's feet. "You mustn't talk like that. You know he'll get all right."

Ethel went on stirring outwardly calm, but a tear escaped and rolled down her cheek.

"I wouldn't say this to another living soul but you, Annabel, but I'm not sure. He's been a bad colour for some time now."

"But, mum, it's not like you to give way."

"Nor it is." Ethel tried to square her shoulders. "The truth is I was already a bit down and didn't need any more pushing."

"Lorna?"

"Yes." Ethel swallowed the last of her cocoa. "I've had a letter from her teacher. Very nice, mind you, but she says it's making her difficult-tempered being here where everyone knows, and she ought to get away."

"That's what David said." Annabel could have kicked herself. What had made her talk of David? Why hurt herself more than she need?

"Did he?" Ethel smiled. "Sensible sort. Shouldn't wonder if he had bright ideas."

"Oh, he had." Annabel could not resist adding a dash of paint to her lily. "He said he had a lodge-keeper's wife who would like to have her."

"I dare say. But where's the money coming from?" Ethel got up. "Well, I must go up to Dad." She put her arm round Annabel. "I can't thank you enough. I was wondering, do you think if you told Miss Petoff how things were she'd let you off early so as to come with Dad and me to the hospital?" She gave a rather ashamed smile. "Matter of fact, it's not so much for Dad. That first night without him, leaving him there, I feel I would like to have you. Old silly, aren't I?"

"Course not. I'll ask Miss Petoff. You go up to dad. I'll just rinse out these cups."

Left to herself Annabel turned on the tap. She picked the mop from the jar and slowly spun it inside a cup. Round and round it went. The cup could not have been cleaner, but still it twirled.

Was it possible, she thought, that life could ever be happy again? Was it possible that some day she would forget and either love someone else, or at least not mind so much? They said time healed anything, but here was Wednesday and she didn't feel a bit better than she had on Sunday night. She thought of her Mother. Alfie's illness. Lorna. Now Dad. Was loving worth while? Perhaps not. Perhaps there were too many hurts. Perhaps she was lucky it was finished for her. Suddenly, savagely, she pushed the cup on to the side of the sink. Lucky! For five minutes of David a whole life time of unhappiness would be worth while. What was the good of pretending. Why try and fool yourself? It didn't help really. Nothing helped. She gulped. Wiped and hung up the cups, turned out the light, and went to bed.

Fright hangs about the solar plexus like a balloon. No matter what you are doing you feel its pressure. That was how it was at the Brown's that Wednesday morning. Ethel, apparently composed, poured out the tea and helped the bacon and eggs. She took a small portion of bacon herself, but she pushed the teapot between her plate and the children. She knew Annabel would not expect her to be eating, but she did not want the others calling attention to her lack of appetite. Alfie did his best to lighten the gloom but his effort was not happy.

"I hope we have the lilies ready for Dad."

"Why!" Ethel exclaimed.

"Well for him to see when he comes out of hospital."

"Of course, Son," Ethel agreed apologetically.

"What did you think he meant, Mum?" Lorna asked. Then the possible purpose of lilies came to her. "You don't mean—"

"Of course Mum meant nothing," Annabel said firmly. She fumbled desperately for a change of subject. "Tell you what would be nice, if we could have Mum's curtains up before Dad gets home."

"Gosh, yes." Alfie agreed. "Do let's try. It would be a surprise for him. Though perhaps it would be better to have new ones in his bedroom."

Ethel poured herself out another cup of tea.

"Why dear?"

"Well, he's likely to be there a lot isn't he?"

Annabel gave a sympathetic glance at her Mother.

"What rot you talk, Alfie. By the time Dad comes home he'll be sick of bed. What he'll want to do is to lie outside in the sun and have a look at his garden."

Such a vision, with herself running to and fro with cushions and nourishment was almost too much for Ethel. She took refuge behind a fixed mechanical grin.

"There's some lovely pots of hyacinths going cheap at a shop near school," said Alfie. "I'm going to buy one to take Dad on visiting day. Which days can you visit there, Annabel?"

Lorna helped herself to some jam.

"Any day if he's on the danger list."

Annabel would have liked to have slapped her.

"Well Dad's not going on any danger list and Mum and I will find out about ordinary visiting when we're there to-night." She got up and kissed her mother. "So long, Mum. See you at the hospital."

The model room had changed since Bernadette had left. Freda and Elizabeth had always been friends. In Bernadette's day they had made a semblance of "All girls together." But with only Annabel to compete with they stopped bothering.

These last two days they had only talked to each other, except when Freda cross-examined Annabel as to Bernadette's whereabouts. Annabel had been far too depressed to want to talk to them, but even in her state of gloom the changed atmosphere of the room permeated. So it was with surprise that she found herself greeted cheerfully by Freda.

"Hullo. Where were you off to in a hurry in a taxi last night?"

Annabel had nothing to hide.

"I went to see Mr. Offenbach. Something to do with my father."

"Your father!" Freda's mouth opened and a howl of laughter came out. "Your father. That's a good one."

Annabel had just taken off her frock. She stood with it in one hand staring at Freda. Slowly what little colour she had drained from her face. She was not a person who lost her temper easily but when she lost it, she lost it utterly. What could Freda find funny in her Dad. She came slowly across the room.

"If you want to know I went to see Mr. Offenbach to see if he could get my father into St. Thomas's Hospital. He goes in to-night, they'll operate to-morrow. It isn't funny." She gave Freda a well placed, well timed slap on the face. Then without a word picked up her dressing-gown and went out of the room.

Elizabeth looked in a flabbergasted way at the door, then at Freda who had sunk, with her head in her hands, shaking into her chair.

"Who'd have thought she had it in her. You'll report her to Miss Petoff of course." She knelt beside Freda. "Don't cry."

"Cry!" Freda looked up, tears of laughter streaming down her face. "That's handed me the best laugh I've had in years."

"Why?"

Freda choked back her amusement and looked at Elizabeth.

"Can I trust you?"

Elizabeth licked a finger.

"See this wet, see this dry, cut my throat, if I lie. Go on."

Freda pulled herself together and mopped her eyes.

"I knew she'd been to Ossy's last night, but of course I never thought of the hospital. You know she's been out with David de Bett. Well of course the Glaye doesn't like it, as she wants to marry him. So I rung our dear Octavia up last night and said I'd a bit of news about Annabel which would put dear David off her forever. She said: 'Come round.' And I said: 'Only if I get ten pounds.'"

"And did you?"

Freda opened her bag and took out a pair of fivers which she dangled in front of Elizabeth's nose.

"I did. And it was all about a hospital. Is that rich? Will Octavia foam at the mouth when she knows. Hold me up."

Elizabeth appreciated the joke. The two girls rocked.

Miss Bell looked sourly round the door.

"Is no work being done this morning? Freda, there's a customer to see the jade chiffon."

Freda waited till the door was shut, then she went to the corner cupboard.

"A bit early but I think this deserves a bromo seltzer."

David on the road to London gave himself up to worried thinking. What was Annabel doing with Ossy Offenbach? Had Octavia made it up? It was not likely, if she was going to make up a tale like that she would hardly produce a name. But Annabel had no friends of his sort, not that he believed all the rubbish talked about Ossy's nieces, his own belief was that Ossy's connection with his nieces was philanthropic. All the same he did not like it for Annabel. Why had she become a niece? If she was hard up couldn't she have come to him. Silly little fool getting herself talked about. Of coursed there was probably a perfectly good explanation of the friendship which she would tell him, but he did wish that nobody could say such things about her. Coming on top of what she had said the other night it left an unpleasant taste in the mouth.

Arrived at his flat he wrote a note:

My dear Annabel,
It seems you and I have a nice bit of talking to do. I had the enclosed from Octavia. If you have nothing on your conscience, will you step into my car at six, and we could have an early bite.
Yours, David.

He took the note to Bertna's himself. He gave it to the commissionaire who in return for half a crown assured him Miss Brown was in, and he would put it into her hands himself.

It was some hours until six. David felt restless; he decided that, though he would certainly play vilely, golf would probably distract him better than anything. He turned his car out of London.

Annabel had been showing a rose net evening frock. She had managed to give an affect of gaiety, which the frock called for, while in the showroom, but outside her shoulders drooped. Would this wretched day never end. Miss Petoff had been charming and said of course she could leave early, but that would not be till teatime, and the morning wasn't over yet. It was awful of her to have hit Freda, but she had no right to laugh at Dad being ill. Of course she and Elizabeth weren't saying anything but they would go to Miss Petoff and then she would get dismissed, and that would be another worry for Mum, as if Dad being ill wasn't enough.

"Hi!"

Annabel looked round and saw the commissionaire.

"Did you want me?"

The commissionaire looked hurt.

"I don't walk up and down stairs for the pleasure of wearing out me heart." He held out David's letter. "Gent in a car brought this. Said it was to be put into your hands. Most particular he was. You'll put it right into Miss Brown's hands won't you, he says."

"Thank you, Thompson." Annabel took the letter. She stood looking at the envelope. Thompson cleared his throat as if to say more, then seeing that she was blind and deaf, plodded back to his post.

Almost afraid to breathe, Annabel split the envelope.

She drew out the two letters. She saw one was addressed to David, it was the other which made her heart stand still. "Yours David". And she had never expected to hear from him again.

In her first reading of the letter she paid no attention to the line about the enclosed from Octavia. "You and I have a nice bit of talking to do." That sentence was the opening of the gates of Paradise. If she might talk to him perhaps she could explain, make him see. Even the cryptic line, "If you have nothing on your conscience" did not trouble her. David knew all she had on her conscience. Her cheap silly outlook which had almost killed their friendship. She read the letter again. This time there was a faint pucker between her eyes.

She had remembered about to-night. She would not be able to step into his car at six. Considering this awful thought she turned towards the models' room. Then remembered Octavia's letter. She pulled it out of its envelope.

There are some slanders too silly to matter. That was how Annabel first treated what Octavia said. Then suddenly it dawned on her why David had sent her the letter. "You and I have a nice bit of talking to do." "If you have nothing on your conscience—" Octavia had written this thing and he wanted to hear from her, Annabel, that it wasn't true. And she couldn't be here at six to tell him. But she must be. She was sorry about Dad, and hated to let Mum down, but this might mean her whole happiness. They couldn't expect her to risk it. She was being given a second chance, she would be mad not to take it. But even as she thought this she remembered Ethel's words. "I wouldn't say this to another living soul. I'm not sure. He's a bad colour." Poor Mum scared to go home alone. Afraid of her thoughts. It was only one night she asked for help. By to-morrow they would know. Even if the news was bad it would be easier than uncertainty. Though to Annabel death was an incredible thing which happened to other people, but not to her family, she could just grasp that to Ethel there would be relief in knowing exactly what she had to face. To-night she could not have that relief and she wanted her daughter with her. Even if she spoilt her whole life because of it Annabel knew she couldn't let her down. Six o'clock must come and she let her chance go by.

Freda and Elizabeth were showing. Annabel, taking off her frock and pulling on her dressing-gown considered what she should say. She must of, course telephone and tell David not to come. But after what she had said the other night, and what Octavia said now, it wasn't very easy to know what opening thing to say. Just hearing his voice was sure to make her stupid. Of course they'd say: "Hullo" and that seemed idiotic seeing how she felt. And then she'd have to say "I'm so sorry I can't come to-night" and then explain about Dad, and then explain how kind Mr. Offenbach had been, and then say how sorry she was about Sunday. She took a deep breath and got two pennies out of her bag.

"Is that Grosvenor 2970? Oh, is Lord de Bett there?" The man-servant's voice did not sound very friendly.

"His Lordship is out. Is there any message?"

Annabel clutched the receiver tightly. She had a feeling if she did not the man would go away.

"But I must speak to him. What time will he be in?"

The man-servant was now definitely disapproving.

"I couldn't say I'm sure. But not till late. His Lordship expected to be out until after dinner. What name shall I say?"

"None." Annabel replaced the receiver. "His Lordship expected to be out until after dinner!" That meant he was away for the day and was coming straight from wherever he was to fetch her. She couldn't speak to him. Couldn't even send him a note by messenger. She would have to leave a letter for him here. But who would give it to him? Thompson was always gone before six. If only Bernadette were still here. It would have to be either Freda or Elizabeth. They both knew him try sight. On the whole she thought Freda would be safest, she would do anything for money. She went back to the models' room. To her surprise the other two were still away. She had a block of note-paper, and a fountain pen. She curled up in her chair.

Dear David,

I am so sorry I can't come to dinner with you tonight, but I have to go with Mum to the hospital, as Dad is having an operation to-morrow. It is quite true I went to see Mr. Offenbach. I went to ask him to get Dad into a hospital and he has. I think he is the kindest man I ever knew.

I am sorry I was so stupid on Sunday.

Annabel.

She was not very pleased with this effort. It read coldly, but she did not know how to say how miserable she had been; besides, he might not like it. She folded the paper and put it in an envelope. She licked every inch of gum on the flap, and when she had fixed it down, sat on it, to be sure it was secure. She had no illusions about Freda; if she could open the letter and read it she would.

Freda and Elizabeth were in deep consultation outside the showroom door.

"After all," Elizabeth whispered, "I saw her hit you. She can't say she didn't do it. She's never been our sort. Let's take the chance to get rid of her. We mightn't get it again. It's a pretty thing if us girls get hit every time we open our mouths."

Freda considered the point. She did not want Annabel in the models' room. On the other hand, she had been a nice source of income. Fifteen pounds all told, which was a pleasant picking. The question was, would she be worth any more? It was almost certain David de Bett would find out what Annabel had been to see Ossy Offenbach about, and would pass it on to Octavia, who could hardly help feeling she had been done. In fact, it was almost certain that

Octavia would be furious and refuse any more news she might pick up. Really, taking it by and large, she did not see how Annabel could be much more good. She had better go.

"Right. You pop back to our room and I'll tell the Gale I want to see Miss Petoff."

Miss Gale felt that her mission in life was to keep trouble from Tania.

"But why do you want to see Miss Petoff? What is it about?"

Freda knew her rights.

"Miss Petoff makes a rule any of her employees can see her if it's important."

"Well, is it important?"

"Yes."

"All right, Freda. Run back to your work. Miss Petoff is out at present, but I dare say she will spare you two minutes this afternoon."

"Two minutes!" Freda made a face at Miss Gale's back. "Silly old cow. Two minutes!" She'd bet it would take more than that when Miss Petoff heard all she had to say.

Annabel put off giving Freda her letter until the afternoon. She waited for a chance to catch her alone, not that she trusted for a moment that she would not tell Elizabeth, but simply because it was an embarrassing thing to ask, and she thought it would be easier without a third person listening. As it happened, it was a busy afternoon, particularly for herself. There was a rush of dark-haired customers, and until half-past three she seemed to be either showing or changing, and if she were not, then Freda was. But at last there came a moment when they were both resting in their chairs and Elizabeth in the showroom.

"I say, Freda."

Freda looked up from the stocking she was mending. "What?"

"Shall you be in an awful hurry at closing time?"

"Not specially. I'm not going out to dinner until nine. Why?"

"You know Lord de Bett."

"Yes." Not by the flicker of an eyelash did Freda show any undue interest.

"Well, he's calling for me in his car at six. I haven't been able to get hold of him to tell him I'm going to the hospital. Would you give him this letter?" Annabel flushed; she hated the money part. "I'd be glad to pay your taxi home to make up the time you wasted."

"My taxi'll be five bob." Freda held out her hand for the letter.

"All right." Annabel dared not risk giving the money in advance. "I'll give it you in the morning."

Freda's brain was working fast. There ought to be more than five bob in this, if Annabel said the sort of things in that letter she imagined she'd say. She pushed it into her dressing-gown pocket.

"All right."

"You won't forget?" Annabel eyed the pocket doubtfully.

"Forget!" Freda raised one amused, surprised eye. "No, I won't forget."

Miss Gale put her head round the door.

"Freda, Miss Petoff will see you now."

Annabel sat up.

"Freda, are you going to tell her about what I did this morning?"

"Never you mind what I'm seeing her about. That's my business."

"I know." Annabel forgot her shyness in her earnestness. "Only if you have to tell her, please don't ask her to send me away. Not now. You see, father's operation is to-morrow, and we don't know how it'll turn out. I may need the money very badly."

Freda went to the door.

"Your family affairs are your business. It's my duty to tell Miss Petoff what happened; what she does about it is up to her."

"Well, Freda?" Tania looked up from the cheque she was signing. "I hear you want to see me."

"Yes, Miss Petoff. I thought I ought to."

"That sounds as if it was going to take time. People who are telling you things because they ought are always long winded." Tania nodded at a chair. "Sit down."

Annabel was in a quandary. She had been told she might leave at half-past four. But Freda was still with Miss Petoff and Elizabeth had been sent for. She was the only one left. She looked anxiously at her watch. She couldn't keep Dad waiting; she had better get dressed. Perhaps if a customer came in they would get Freda or Elizabeth. Of course it would be very unlucky if something wanted showing and they found her dressed. Probably even at this minute Miss Petoff was deciding to give her notice, and her being dressed when she was needed would not help. She had just put on her hat when Miss Gale came in. Annabel flushed and started.

"I'm sorry. But Miss Petoff said I could go early. I can undress in a minute."

Miss Gale smiled kindly.

"It's all right, dear. I hear your father is ill. I am so sorry. I hope you have good news tomorrow. Miss Petoff wants to see you."

Annabel appreciated the kindness much as a condemned man must appreciate being allowed to choose his breakfast on his last morning. All the same, it was nice of Miss Gale to be sorry for her. She was not the sort of person who ever got notice, so it was kind of her to be sorry for people who did.

"I'd better take my coat and things, then I can go at once." Miss Gale nodded.

"Yes, Miss Petoff told me to tell you to come down ready to leave."

"Yes." Sadly Annabel pulled on her coat and picked up her bag and gloves. "I'm ready."

Freda sat on one side of Tania's desk, Elizabeth on the other. Annabel, shaking at the knees, stood in the door. Tania looked up at her. She did not smile.

"Come in, Annabel. Is it true you hit Freda this morning?"

Annabel gulped; she felt as if her voice was leaving her. "Yes."

"Why did you do it?"

"Because she laughed because my father was ill."

"What!" Tania turned to Freda. "This is not what you told me."

Freda flushed.

"It isn't true."

"Oh, Freda!" Annabel looked shocked. "You know it is. You asked me where I'd been, and when I said I'd been to see Mr. Offenbach for my father, you laughed."

"You never said he was ill."

Tania held up her hand.

"What was there to laugh at, whether her father was ill or well?"

Freda looked at Elizabeth. They giggled.

"Well, you know," Freda explained, "what he is. I thought it was a bit of a long story, and so it was."

Tania beckoned to Annabel.

"Why did you go to see Mr. Offenbach? Did you know him?"

"No, but, you see, someone where Dad worked died in our hospital and Mum thought it would be better if Dad went somewhere else. She asked me if I would ask—would ask somebody." Annabel paused, breathless.

"Go on," said Tania gently.

"Well, I didn't know anyone to ask. But on Monday that Miss Rose White, Mr. Offenbach's new niece"—a smile flickered across Tania's mouth—"she came in and she saw I was upset and asked me why, and when I told her, she said she'd ask him to help me. His secretary rang up on Tuesday morning and said he'd see me. I went. He was kinder than anybody I ever knew. He's got Dad into St. Thomas's and—" The clock on Tania's desk struck the half hour. Half-past four. Dad even now on his way. Annabel choked. Her eyes filled with tears.

Tania got up. She came round from behind the desk and put an arm round Annabel. She gave her a squeeze.

"Run along, my child. You can't go round the world hitting people, but this time you'll not hear another word about it."

The door shut on Annabel. Tania leant against it. She looked at Freda with dislike.

"Aren't you a cad? Have you no imagination?" Then she looked at Elizabeth. "I know you've none, but must you lie? Why did you tell me that Annabel hit Freda with no provocation? No provocation! Good God!" She came back to her chair and tapped her blotter thoughtfully. "I'm giving you both a week's notice. There's no hardship in it. You are both lovely and will get new jobs in a moment. But as far as I'm concerned, Bertna's only employs the best. You two may come up to that standard outwardly, but inwardly I should think only you two know just how short you fall. Now run along; there may be a customer waiting."

"Sacked!" Freda helped herself to a bromo seltzer. "Sacked!"

"Oh, well," Elizabeth filed her nails, "I was thinking of making a change soon, anyway."

"Liar!" Freda gave her drink a stir. Then suddenly a light came into her eye. She felt in her pocket. "For once little Freda is not going to be mercenary." She put down her glass and drew out the letter. Deliberately she tore it in pieces.

Elizabeth looked up.

"What's that?"

Freda put the fragments of the letter in an envelope.

"Something for our Annabel to find in the morning." She took a gulp of her drink. "I'd just love to think I'd nipped that affair in the bud, blast her!"

Thursday morning was wet. It did not need the sight of the rain to add to the depression of waking. Ethel had been splendid; while she was conscious she kept a brave face. But in bed she dropped off into snatches of sleep and then the horrors got her. Three times Annabel went to her in answer to a cry to find the sound had been made while she was asleep, and had not only woken her, but woken her in a state of shivering fright. At the third call Annabel stayed.

"Don't be frightened to drop off, Mum. I'm here."

Annabel and Ethel were not the only ones to stare with eyes heavy from want of sleep at the wet pavements. David had sat up all night. So Annabel had something on her conscience. There was something between her and Ossy Offenbach. And who else? It was incredible. He would have sworn by all his gods that Annabel would at least have seen him and faced his accusation. But she had not. She had slipped off before six to avoid him. But she shouldn't. She should hear what he had to say. He'd make her listen. Worthless little wretch. He would see her at lunch-time to-day if he had to break into the shop to do it. Then he would go back to Lunge and stop there. His mother could talk of marriage till her head blew off. He had seen all he wanted to of girls for a bit. First that cheap gold-digger Octavia, and now Annabel—Annabel who had seemed innocent as a cowslip. God, he'd been a fool, but a bloke didn't lay himself out to be hurt twice. He was through.

Ethel was running. Her hat was on one side and wisps of hair blew across her nose. She ran against the pedestrian traffic up Piccadilly, up Bond Street, round to Hanover Square. As she ran she was jostled and pushed, but she did not notice. She was completely unconscious that people stared; she could not see them, for her eyes were dim with tears. Still running, she reached Bertna's. She caught hold of Thompson.

"Is Annabel Brown in?"

Thompson looked apologetically at the other occupier of the steps.

"She is; this gentleman is waiting for her."

Ethel turned and saw David. Her face lit up.

"You! I might have known. I wondered how Annabel was able to keep so calm these last days. But of course you'd be a wonderful help."

"If you are waiting for Annabel," said David coldly, "I'll go."

"No." Ethel caught his arm. "You tell her. Tell her it was nothing malignant, and Dad's come through the operation wonderfully. They're so nice at the hospital, you ask her just to ring up Mr. Offenbach and give him a thank you from us all."

Annabel came down the steps. David took her hands.

"Darling, I don't know what it's all about, but your mother's been here; she says your father's come through the operation wonderfully, and it wasn't malignant and—" He caught hold of her.

"My sweet, don't faint. It's good news. Come on, I'll help you into the car."

After a pause Annabel said:

"I'm sorry about Sunday."

He took his hand off the steering wheel and squeezed hers. "I think it's I who ought to be sorry. Why can't I say straight out what I mean?"

"What was it you wanted to show me in your flat?"

He gave her a quick look.

"Like to come and see before lunch?"

She nodded.

"Please."

David stopped his car in Mount Street. He took Annabel's hand and led her up to his flat. He put her on a sofa.

"Do you remember my quoting to you 'For what they'd never told me of, and what I never knew'?"

"Yes. You said if I found what it came from I'd know what it meant. But I never found it."

He ran his finger to and fro across his books.

"It's Rupert Brooke." He picked out a volume and searched through it. He passed it open to Annabel. "There you are. Read the last verse."

Annabel read:

> "And so I never feared to see,
> You wander down the street,
> Or come across the fields to me
> On ordinary feet.
> For what they'd never told me of,
> And what I never knew,
> It was that all the time, my love,
> Love would be merely you."

Annabel looked up.

"You wanted me to come up to show me this?"

"Yes."

"What a beast you must have thought me!"

He sat beside her and took her in his arms.

"Such a nice little beast. Will you marry me?"

Annabel nodded.

"I'll be frightened, and unsuitable, but I'll never love anyone else, so I must."

"Unsuitable!" He kissed her. "Awful fate to marry a snob."

CHAPTER TWELVE

THE lilies were out. Not the twelve that George had bought, nor yet the riot that Ethel had dreamed. But what even the most envious neighbour had to admit was "a fine show," and what to Ethel, standing spellbound before such silver whiteness and scent, seemed too much loveliness to show a woman whose heart was already bursting with happiness.

"Look at you," said Lorna. "Thought you went out to arrange the cushions, not to admire the garden."

Alfie hung out of the window.

"Well, it's worth admiring, isn't it?"

Ethel looked up, smiling. Alfie looked so well. She could not remember a summer when he had looked like that before the holiday.

"Bring out the table, son."

Maudie came running.

"Mum, can I help?"

"Course you can, pet." Ethel handed the child the cushions she was holding. "You set them on the couch while I get the tea ready."

Lorna turned into the house.

"I'll bring out the chairs."

Ethel flushed. She dare not say anything. Lorna, being nice for almost the first time since her trouble, was filling her cup too full.

Annabel was in the kitchen.

"You run along, Mum, and smell the lilies. You leave the tea to me."

Ethel took hold of the knife with which Annabel was spreading the butter.

"Kitchen's no place for a future peeress."

Annabel retrieved her knife.

"Silly." Then she looked at Ethel and giggled.

"Just think of me being called m'lady, and spoken of as her ladyship. I can't help laughing each time I think of it."

"Well, all marriages have their trials." Ethel fetched the tea tin. "I'd find that a pretty big one, same as I would having all those servants. I'd hate another woman having her say-so in my kitchen. But you can get used to anything.

That's what I said to Dad when I married him. He said he was a bit of a stick-in-the-mud, and would never make a fortune." Ethel turned to have a look at the kettle. "I said, 'Well, I never cared for mud, but if you like sticking in it, I'll get used to it.'" Her voice softened. "And so I have."

"Mum! Mum!" Lorna, Alfie and Maudie all screaming together. "He's come."

There was a wild rush to the door. Alfie had a start, but somehow it was Ethel who got to the gate first. She had her arms out to George as David helped him from his car.

George was thin. The hand resting heavily on his stick was a bit transparent. But there was a faint sunburn on his cheeks. He straightened his back.

"What do you think of that? Not much of an invalid, is there?" He smiled affectionately at David. "Wonderful what a bit of Lunge air can do, isn't it, David?"

"Did you enjoy yourself, Dad?"

"Did you see the ghost?"

"Did you eat strawberries out of the garden?" Ethel silenced the children with a smile and took George's arm.

"Tea's in the garden. Come on."

George gave her elbow a squeeze—a squeeze that said "Lunge was fine, but what I needed was home and you."

They all watched George when he had the first sight of his lilies. They were not disappointed. Those weeks in the hospital there had never been a flower come into the ward but he wondered how they were getting on. Down at Lunge he had admired, but he had watched the gardeners at work with a scornful gleam in his eye. What did a man know of pleasure in a garden unless every plant was thought out, and took a bit of sacrifice to get, and a bit of love in the putting into the ground. Driving up from Sussex, George had thought about his lilies. Would they be out? Not all of course but perhaps one or two. But they were all out, and more. He turned an accusing eye on Ethel.

"I put in twelve."

"Maybe they've doubled themselves." Ethel suggested.

George shook his head.

"Own up. Where did you get the money?"

Alfie hopped across the lawn.

"Curtain box, Mum?"

Ethel pulled George's arm.

"You come on the couch, Mr. Inquisitive."

George shook his head sadly at Alfie and Lorna.

"She'll never get those curtains."

Tea was over. A cheerful laughing tea. Ethel tried to keep the children quiet because of tiring George, but she did not succeed. Anyway George did not look tired. He lay staring at his lilies, the picture of content.

"Now I've brought the master of the house home," David said to Ethel, "How about the date of our wedding?"

Ethel fidgeted with her fingers.

"Yes. We ought to fix that, David."

David laid his hand on hers.

"Don't want to let her go just yet?"

Ethel looked up.

"No. I shall miss her. But she'll be happy with you. I know that. It's only—"

George caught David's eye. He pulled himself up a bit on the couch.

"David and I have been talking about this wedding while I was at his place. So did Annabel when she was down, didn't you, my girl?"

Annabel got up and came and sat at her mother's feet.

"You know, Mum, when I got engaged you talked of a wedding from here?"

"And so it's going to be." Ethel said quickly. "We may not have much money, but when my girls marry, they'll marry from their own home."

"I know." Annabel agreed. "But I told Dad I believed you were worrying about it. And you were too."

"No." Ethel shook her head. "But it can't be done in a rush."

David got up and hung over the back of her chair. "That's just the trouble. I want to rush. So would any man who was marrying Annabel."

Ethel looked up at him. Her eyes were sympathetic but she shook her head.

"If you think you're going to soft soap me into allowing you to spend your money on a big wedding at a smart hotel you're much mistaken, young man."

"Mum." Annabel looked quite shocked. "I'd hate to be married in a smart hotel. I don't want a lot of people staring." She flushed. "It would take some of the loveliness away if there was anybody in the church who wasn't fond of us."

Her tone moved David. He was bound to joke not to show what he felt.

"Just fancy. And I had planned to have Freda and Elizabeth in the front row."

"Those two!" Ethel's voice put them both where she felt they belonged. "But if you don't want that sort of wedding what do you want? Neither Dad nor I would stand for a registry office."

"Nor would I." Annabel fumbled with Ethel's fingers. "David thought perhaps you would let us be married in his own village church." Her voice grew warm. "Mum, it's so lovely. Very old with memorials to all his family round the walls. Then the village people could come and the servants, and all of you and Bernadette and her husband—"

"And just my very nicest relations." David broke in. "And if so, what about August?"

Ethel looked at George. It was true arranging this wedding had worried her. Weddings cost such a lot. All the same a girl ought to be married from her home. But one glance at George settled the matter. It was obvious what he wished.

"Very well," she agreed. "August."

"Weddin' in August," Maudie piped out. "Can I be a bridesmaid an' wear blue?"

"And can I be a bridesmaid and wear pink?" Lorna implored.

Alfie picked a grass and stuck it behind his ear.

"And Alfie will wear white satin and be a page."

How they all laughed. The thought of tall Alfie dressed like that made them roll about. When they stopped laughing they found Annabel and David had gone. Lorna was the first to notice it.

"Goodness, Annabel and David have gone in. Soppy things."

Ethel looked at George and they remembered a day when they had always been slipping off.

"Puts us in mind of a time," Ethel whispered.

George slipped his hand over hers.

"Mum, Mum. Could you come in a minute."

They looked up. Annabel was leaning out of the window.

Alfie nudged Lorna. Lorna took Maudie by the hand. They crept after Ethel.

"Come on, Mum." Annabel's voice came from the sitting room. Puzzled, Ethel, hurried in. In the doorway she stood gasping.

There are curtains and curtains. The ones that Annabel and David had chosen were even, lovelier than those she had seen in the shop before Maudie was born. The same green, but such velvet! Never had Ethel dreamed of owning curtains of material like that. Why it must have cost pounds a yard. She went over and felt them admiringly, but her eyes were stern.

"Annabel, you shouldn't have let him. You know I wouldn't like him spending all that money on me."

David put his arm round Annabel. He picked up her left hand and held it out. On the first finger there were a small cluster of emeralds.

"It wasn't me. You see that ring. The one I chose was quite different. A single emerald costing quite a lot of money. Annabel saw it and said: 'Take that back. It's a waste. What I'd like is a cheap ring and the difference to send Lorna to boarding school, and if there's a bit over let's get Mum her velvet curtains.'"

Lorna screamed and threw herself on them both. Ethel's head was turned away. She still held the curtain.

George came in.

"What is it? I'm not such an invalid that I'm going to be kept out of things." Then he saw the curtains. "The green velvet curtains!" He nodded at Ethel. "She opened that box at last? I always knew there was money in it."

"Money!" Ethel turned round and they saw she was crying. Annabel took her arm.

"What is it, Mum?"

Ethel tossed her head.

"I didn't cry when Fordwych's cut the wages, nor when Alfie was so bad, nor that winter when you all nearly died of the 'flu, and not much when you gave us the fright of our lives." She grinned at George. Her eye roved over Lorna, and rested on Annabel's.

THE END

FURROWED MIDDLEBROW

*titles available in paperback only
**pseudonym of Noel Streatfeild